ABSINTHE

ROBIN H SOPRANO

Absinthe by Robin H. Soprano

Copyright © 2015 by Robin Soprano

Cover layout by Alexandra King

Absinthe by Robin H. Soprano

270p. ill. cm.

ISBN 978-1-935795-40-7
LCCN

Michael Ray King Publishing
PO Box 353431
Palm Coast, FL 32135-3431

Printed in the United States of America

Author's Notes & Dedications...

Thank you to all of my supporting friends. You all keep me going!

Special thanks to:

Author/publisher Michael Ray King: For listening, helping, encouraging, and above all, keeping my inner critic quiet.

Author Carol V. Aebersold: For beta reading and your sharp eye and insight. I appreciate all and any advice. I value our friendship always.

Margherita Perry: For beta reading everything I write, for truthful insights, for helpful ideas, and promoting my books. I know you always have my back.

Susan Kework: For beta reading my work and always being intrigued by my writing. You are motivation at its finest. Keep it up.

Author Jorja Dupont Oliva: For sharing ideas and helping me push through writer's slump. And for making me see things inside out with a different light. You inspire and enlighten.

Editor Karin Nicely: You are the mirror to my words and helped to establish the magic in them.

Paul and my family: Thanks for the wonderful support.

Alexa Miller: For spending a day with me and taking photos and helping me create cover art. You brought my idea to life; you have great patience.

Alexandra King: For putting my book cover together and making it a reality!

All of my Author Friends near and far: For your friendship, kind words, advice, and chats. It all helps one way or another. I am surrounded by many talented writers, poets, and dreamers.

~ *ABSINTHE* ~

By: Robin H. Soprano

CHAPTER ONE

We buried Mom next to Daddy today.

Sitting in the kitchen of my parents' house, I watch all our friends and family gather together, bringing food and their sympathy. I have just been going through the motions since we all returned here after the cemetery. I have a smile on my face, but I feel miserable, empty, and alone. I feel like an orphan.

After my father died, I came home to Maryland to care for Mom. That's also when I stopped traveling around like a gypsy collecting research for my writing. I've written a few books—romance and mystery. The books are faring well, but I haven't written any more since I've been here with Mom. I struggled to keep writing, but I couldn't, no matter how much I tried.

My sister couldn't help much with Mom, either. She lives about a thousand miles away in Louisiana with her husband and her two kids. They are the owners of a popular bar and restaurant there called Rendezvous. They pack them in almost every night, and my older sister, Charlotte, is the reason. She is an extraordinary chef. Her husband, Jack, tends the bar just like Brian Flanagan in the movie *Cocktail*.

Charlotte and Jack chipped in financially when the old house needed to be fixed here and there, and they never thought twice when I asked for help, but it was mostly me taking care of the household and Mom.

I watch now from a distance as my sister greets and hugs relative after relative. I overhear stories about my parents, processing it all through a foggy haze in my head. My five-year-old niece, Jaqueline, snaps her fingers at me to get my attention.

"AUNTIE SHREE!" her voice pierces through my cloud like a brain-freeze and I look at her through squinty eyes.

"Yes, Jaqueline—what is it?"

"I can't find Fweedo. Did you see him go fwoo here?" Her hands raise and her baby-blue eyes grow bigger as she looks for Friedo, her little bichon frise puppy.

"No, sweetie. Maybe your brother has him outside. Go check there."

"K!" she answers.

Jaqueline takes off through the back door to where her older brother, Charlie, has been most of the day, sulking. My guess is that the poor kid was just trying to comprehend the whole death thing. Watching his parents and me shed tears was probably unnerving, to say the least, and at the tender age of ten he was in that crazy preteen-angst stage, anyway.

A few more hours pass, and we're finally saying our goodbyes to the last of Mom's cousins and starting to tidy up the house before bedtime.

"I'm exhausted!" I say to Charlotte as I fall onto the sofa, putting my feet on the worn-out hassock.

"Me, too, Sharie. Jesus, what a day!" my sister huffs as she plops down next to me.

"Where's Jack?" I ask.

"Upstairs with the kids and Friedo, trying to settle them down." She put her hand on my leg and loudly exhaled. "We are it, now, sister. We just have us."

"Yep," I say quietly, nodding my head in agreement.

We turn as we hear Jack trotting down the stairs. The old wood still squeaks in the same places that had gotten my sister and me in trouble as teenagers when we tried to sneak in or out of the house. Daddy caught us most of the time.

"All right, the kids are clean and in bed. Friedo, too. What are you girls talking about?"

"Nothing much," I answer, "Just that we're all that's left." I point to myself and Charlotte.

Jack looks at us with a sad smile. He has a five-o'clock shadow and looks as tired as my sister and I. As if a light bulb is going off in his head, he raises his eyebrows over his tired, blue eyes and holds up a finger. "I have a really good idea, Sharie. Why don't you sell this house and come live out near us. That way, we can all be together, closer, and you know the kids would love it."

"I agree!" Charlotte pipes in. "What do you think, Sharie? You would love it by us. You know we're close to New Orleans, so you can get your culture and art, maybe get inspired to write a few more books! Your last ones look

3

like they are doing pretty well. I check their progress all the time."

I laugh, "They're not doing as good as I wanted, but I can't complain." I look at them quizzically. "You guys really think I should? It does sound nice to be near you and the kids."

"Okay, then!" Jack claps his hands together once. "We'll call a realtor first thing tomorrow."

***

After a few short months, our old house had sold and within the same few months I found an old but well-preserved manor that was a steal. The house is twenty minutes from Charlotte's and Jack's place and about twenty minutes outside New Orleans. I can't believe my luck!

The manor had been a vacation home for an English family, passed down to them from an ancestor who had it built in the 1800s, but unfortunately they just no longer had time for it and wanted to get rid of it. The house is beautiful, built with stone and an asymmetrical, sloping roof. With its small-paned casement windows and two chimneys, the house looks like something out of a fairy tale. I am enchanted.

On the inside, a long, narrow staircase takes a slight turn to a landing with three big bedrooms and a bathroom. The master bedroom has its own fireplace and private bathroom.

Downstairs, on the second floor, the kitchen has been modernized without spoiling its original charm. It shares a double-sided fireplace with the massive living room, but the dining room is smaller and separate. A door from the kitchen opens to a small landing and then stairs leading down to a patio and the expansive back yard.

The first floor is partially below and partially opening out to ground level. It has its own entrance in the back of the house and windows that overlook the patio garden. That level is where I decide to make my office, where I will write. I just want to make a few changes, so the remodelers I've hired are scheduled to begin a week after I move in.

***

It is now a rainy Saturday afternoon in March. Charlotte drops the kids off while she is running some errands, and I let them help unpack a few boxes. We start with the ones that hold family pictures. I grab a hammer and some nails, and we find a good, plain wall where we can hang most of the various photos of us all. Some of them, I decide, could go on the beautiful mantelpiece above the stone fireplace in the living room.

"Aunt Shree," Jaqueline says as she points at a photo, "here's one of Mommy and you. Mommy had long hair. Why did she cut it?"

I look at the picture and remember when it was taken. Charlotte had long, golden, wavy hair and has hazel eyes. I have straight, light-brown hair that pokes out every chance it gets and light-brown eyes. When I was growing up, I had always felt like the plain Jane next to my sister. "Your mommy cut her hair after she became a chef, sweetie, but it's still pretty, don't you think?"

Jaqueline looks again at the photo, studying it, and shrugs her shoulder.

The kids ask many questions about almost every picture and want a story about every one of them. I show them our school pictures, and photos of their grandparents and great-grandparents. Charlie understands the relationships more than Jaqueline, but I figure she'll ask again in a few years.

"Hello! I'm back!" Charlotte yells from the back doorway that opens into the kitchen.

"We're in here, Char!" I call back to her.

"Well, what's going on in here?" she asks.

"Picture hanging," I answer, holding up a hammer.

"Hey, Mom!" Charlie looks up from a pile of photo albums. "Aunt Sharie is telling us all about our family and telling us stories about you growing up!"

"She is, is she...?" My sister looks at me with worried and quizzical eyes.

"Don't worry, Char. I'm not that stupid. I'm saving those stories for when they're older." I laugh and wink.

Her face seems to relax, but she rolls her eyes, "I guess paybacks are a bitch."

"Oh yeah, they are!" I laugh.

"Well, you better hurry up and have some kids, Sharie, so I can tell some stories about you, too."

"First, I've got to find a man. That's the hardest part."

"You should come and hang out at the restaurant, especially on the weekends. Lots of well-to-do guys come and gather at the bar. You should come by and check it out. It *is* happy hour, after all."

I gaze at my sister's smiling face with her high-hope suggestions. "Not really my thing, Char. You know that. But, I will come and visit and have some of your wonderful meals once in a while, mainly because you and Jack are there."

Charlotte's face droops a little at the corners of her mouth. "You need to get out, Sharie. You're living in a new place, a new state. You need to meet people, make some friends."

"Whoa! I just got here. Let me get my feet on the ground. I'll get there, Char. Don't worry about me. I'm okay on my own, and maybe I'll start to travel again."

"No, Aunt Shree, no go! I miss you when you go!" Jaqueline whines and gives me the cutest boo-boo lip ever.

"Yeah, Aunt Sharie," Charlie chimes in. "Don't go away again. When you leave, you're gone for months."

"Hey…okay, guys." I throw my hands in the air in submission. "I'm not going anywhere, yet. Your mom and I are just talking. But come on, guys. It's what I love to do. Someday soon, when you're both older, I will take you on some of my adventures. In the meantime, don't I always bring home really cool stuff for you both?"

"Yes!" they say in unison.

7

"Okay, then, get your stuff. Your mom has to go to work tonight. Thanks for your help, kids!"

"Give Aunt Sharie hugs and kisses goodbye," Char tells her kids then gives me a hug, too. "You want to come by the restaurant later for dinner? I got a shrimp-and-grits special tonight."

"Maybe, but as good as that sounds, I want to go downstairs and see what the carpenters have been up to. Maybe fire up the computer. I finally got cable and internet yesterday, so I should check in with my publisher and look through my email."

"Okay, well, if you change your mind you know that's where we'll be till midnight."

I watch them pull out of the driveway, all waving at me. I return to the task at hand, hanging the last few pictures and arranging them nicely on the wall. I stand back and admire my handiwork. As I take in the sight of my parents and their parents, I shed some tears and think how quickly life seems to pass. I take a deep breath, wipe my face, then trot down the few steps to the first floor. Because of the gloomy day, I flick on some lights. I look around and smile happily at how well the bookshelves are coming along.

I turn on my computer and it hums to life. I check my email, send a few replies, then open the folder that holds some books I'm currently working on. I sit and just draw a blank. After a few hours of staring at nothing on my screen, I shut it down. I think about how my stomach is growling and about the shrimp and grits my sister is preparing. But, in the end, I just want sleep, so early-to-bed trumps dinner, tonight.

***

This morning, Monday, the remodelers arrive again and get to work on my office. I am busying myself with more boxes and cleaning when I hear the owner of the company I hired calling for me.

"Hello? Miss Donovan? You up there?"

"Yes! I'm here. What's up?"

"Can you please come down here? I want you to see something."

I make my way down the steps and look at the four men all standing in front of a wall they've just torn down.

"What's going on? What's the matter?" I ask.

"Miss Donovan, after we cut our way through the wall, we found this." He points to where the wall used to be. Behind it is a previously hidden alcove housing a small desk with a hutch. Within the hutch's nooks and shelves, I see some kind of charm hanging from a chain, some candles, a few small bottles of different-colored powders, and a dusty bottle of green liquid that seemingly was sealed and never opened.

"What the hell is this?" I gesture toward the whole scene.

"Looks like some kind of voodoo stuff, if you ask me," one of the carpenters suggests.

"Voodoo?" I ask, raising my eyebrows. "What the hell does this mean?"

"Well, around these parts, ma'am, voodoo was and still is kind of a big deal, if you believe in that stuff," he answers.

My eyes dart among all four men just standing there, and I notice a name tag that reads "Bobby" on the one who spoke. "Well, Bobby, I don't think I believe it, so I guess we'll just box it all up and put it aside for now."

The owner of the company steps to my side, "The guys don't want to mess too much with it, Miss Donovan. Maybe you should call someone who knows about voodoo stuff and have them take a look at it."

"Oh, come on. You can't be serious." I give all the men another look; they all seem a little apprehensive. I excuse myself for a moment then return carrying an old towel and a nice plastic bin with a lid.

"Whatcha doin', ma'am?" Bobby asks.

"I'm going to box it up and look through it myself." I quickly pull open a few of the desk's drawers. "There's a little notebook here, too, with some writing. If anything, now I'm intrigued. I am a writer, of course, so this is really piquing my interest. And, look at this desk! It must be over a hundred years old. It's an antique, and I'm going to fix it up."

The men stare at me as if I'm nuts.

"I'll be gentle with all of it, I promise," I say, raising my hand like a scout. "I'll even say a prayer before I pack up everything. Would that make you all feel better?" I ask.

All four of them nod.

I put the bin down, lay the towel inside, say a little prayer of protection and a Hail Mary for extra points, and hear a collective "Amen" behind me. Then, slowly I place all the stuff in the box and move the desk out of the way.

Apparently feeling better, the guys get back to work. I proceed to dust off the dark mahogany desk. It's beautiful and polishing up very nicely. I move the bin over to the side and decide to come back and go through it at another time, maybe when the room is finished and the carpenters have gone.

***

It has been a few afternoons since the remodelers found the hidden alcove. Since then, they have applied the first coat of paint, and the room is beginning to look more like a study/library/office. I couldn't be happier with it. The guys are packing up for the day when Bobby looks over at the antique desk.

"Miss Donovan, you decide what you're going to do with the voodoo stuff?"

I look over at the bin and cock my head to the side. "No, Bobby, I haven't. I actually forgot about it; I've been so busy organizing everything. But I'll get to it, I suppose."

"All right, ma'am. You have a good weekend. We should be outta your hair by the middle of next week. We're just about finished," he says as he tips his ball cap.

"Thanks," I answer. "You do the same."

CHAPTER TWO

Now that they've gone, I go back to the alcove and open the plastic storage bin. I find the charm and chain inside and lift it up. It's gold and quite heavy, a cross with roses surrounding it. I figure, how bad can that be, really? It made me feel a little better. I pick up the bottle filled with the green liquid and read the label. It is a little worn, but I can make out the word "Absinthe." I don't recognize the word, but I wonder if it's some sort of liquor and decide my brother-in-law the bartender might know more about it. I'm planning to go to Rendezvous later tonight for dinner, so I'll ask him then.

When I get to the restaurant, the parking lot is nearly full and I can see people at the restaurant's entrance waiting to be seated. I find an empty parking space and pull my old-but-faithful Dodge Durango in. My SUV is getting old, but it got me from Maryland to Louisiana with no problems. Only the outside is getting worn with chips, scratches, and dents.

I walk into the place and it's buzzing with life—music playing, people waiting for tables. At the back bar is where

I spot Jack and another female bartender pouring drinks and handing out beers.

I stand there for a moment, and the host asks if he can help me. I smile. He is young and clean-shaven, well-manicured, and sharply dressed in black trousers and a shiny, purple silk shirt with a black-and-fuchsia tie.

"Hi, I'm Charlotte's sister, Sharie. I was just going back by the bar to see Jack." I held out my hand to him to shake.

"Oh—hi! Nice to finally meet you. I'm Kevin, the host on Thursday, Friday, and Saturday nights. Come with me—they set up a small table just for you. Charlotte told me you were popping in."

"Oh, great, but I don't need a table. I was gonna eat at the bar. You should give the table to paying customers."

"No, no…it's all good, sweetie. Follow me."

I follow Kevin to the back area by the bar where there is a nice, round table that could easily seat about four people and is located strategically close to the kitchen and prep stations, kind of hidden from the view of the dining room.

"See?" Kevin points. "Private family table. Voila!"

"Okay, then, this is great. Thanks, Kevin." I smile.

Kevin helps me with my chair and shoves me in, "Soooo…" he coos. "I have read one of your books!"

"Oh really? Which one?" I smile at his squeaky-clean face.

"*Forever Mated*," he replies and puts his hands to his heart. "My boyfriend and I read it together, and, girl, we just cried…Ah, what a love story."

"I'm so happy you both loved it. Bring it in and I'll sign it for you."

"Oh my God. Truly? You will?" His voice rises and I think he might pass out.

"Yeah, no problem," I answer, laughing with enjoyment at his dramatic reaction.

I watch Kevin sashay away, and I smile at the thought that he has a boyfriend. How nice that he and his partner read a love story together, and how much I want that quality in a man for myself. *Gay couple's love life: 1; Sharie's love life: 0.* I shake my head. At 35, my clock is ticking. I sigh lightly.

"Here you go! A glass of shiraz for my favorite sister-in-law." Jack plants the wineglass in front of me.

"I'm your only sister-in-law," I say sarcastically.

"Okay, true, but you can still be my favorite." He laughs and sits down next to me.

"Don't you have to tend bar? You guys are busy—you don't have to sit with me. I'm fine, really."

"No, it's all good," he says. "We're caught up, and Danielle, there, can handle it. She's good, and the regulars seem to like her. Plus, I own the joint. It's good to be king."

I laugh, "Don't let my sister hear you say that."

"Why? She's the queen, and believe me, she's the ruler around here."

"I believe you," I answer, still smiling.

We order dinner, and I tell Jack to tell my sister whatever she wants to send out for me would be fine. A few minutes later, I get to taste a sample of about six or seven different menu items they had been working on, one more delicious than the next. Jack got up and down from my table but kept me company as best he could. Finally, when the place slowed way down, my sister and Jack both sat with me and poured us some lattes while we had a nibble of dessert.

"How's the office coming along?" Charlotte asks me through the steam of her latte.

"Really good. They painted today, and next week they just need to do the trim and clean up, and that's it. They did an awesome job."

"Good! I'm glad my recommendation is a success," Jack mentions. "The owner is a friend of mine. He and his crew did the work in here, and we are very happy."

"Oh yeah, before I forget…" I interject, changing the subject slightly. "They had to knock down a small wall, and when they did, they found an antique desk with a hutch and some items on it that were of the voodoo nature."

My sister's and brother-in-law's eyes grow wide with interest. "Wow! Really, Sharie? Do you know who it belongs to or where it came from?" Charlotte asks.

"No, but I haven't really looked at everything. Jack"—I point to him—"there is a bottle of what looks like a liquor. The label is old and worn, but it says 'Absinthe' on it. Do you know what that is?"

15

Jack smiles big. "Yes, I do. We have some here. Not many people ask for it. It's a very strong, high-proof alcohol. Anise-flavored, I believe. There has always been a legend about that stuff, but I don't believe any of it. Let me find it—be right back."

He comes back out with a similar but updated bottle of the liquor, some shot glasses, and a few sugar cubes. Using a toothpick, he carefully inserts it into one of the cubes. Suspending the cube with the toothpick across the top of the shot glass, he slowly pours the green liquid over the sugar.

"Here—try this," he says. I pick up the shot and shoot it down. The stuff burns and I cough while my eyes water. Jack shoots one down too, then my sister.

"Holy shit!" Charlotte exclaims. "That could take the paint off a car! That's awful!"

I laugh, "I'll say, but the aftertaste isn't so bad. I do believe it has burned a hole in my stomach, though."

Jack is shaking his head, trying to get rid of the taste. "Yeah, I'll never do that again. Yuck!"

When our taste buds finally come back, I ask what all the fuss is about. "So, what's the deal with this stuff?"

"Legend has it," Jack began, "that it was created in the late eighteenth century by a doctor as an elixir for his patients in Switzerland. The recipe then got into the hands of two sisters who were selling it as a drink in the town. Eventually, it got sold to a family from France who owned a distillery. Somehow, it became associated with drugs. Some say absinthe causes you to hallucinate like heroin. Some say it has psychedelic effects. But it doesn't." Jack chuckles. "Its reputation has been redeemed. It's also known as the 'green fairy,' a mysterious, mythical drink with an incredible history."

"Gee, Jack, you're like a Webster's dictionary of liquor," I say, laughing at him.

"Not really. Just stuff you pick up from years of tending bar, especially in and around New Orleans."

"So, Sharie, what are you going to do with the stuff you found?" my sister asks.

"Don't know, yet." I shrug. "I found a notebook with writing on it, too. I'm definitely intrigued. I'm going to do some snooping, see if I can find something about the house and the original owner."

***

I get home about midnight, put on my jammies, and go to bed, but now I can't sleep. So, I get up, go down to my almost-new office, and turn on my computer. I google "absinthe." What I find online tells me that Jack was pretty much right, but I find more information on the liquor's ingredients: all kinds of herbs, like wormwood, fennel seed, star anise, and more.

Next, I try to find out about the original owner of my house. All I know for sure is that it was built in the 1800s for a family with the surname of Ravensdale, but there the trail goes cold; I figure in the morning I will call the realtor who helped sell me this house and see if she can give me any more information to satisfy my curiosity.

Having exhausted my online resources, I decide to sit on the new wingback chair I bought and look through the voodoo items.

I put the bottle of absinthe on the table and pick up the tiny notebook that seems strangely well preserved for paper with writing on it from over a hundred years ago. I carefully flip through the tiny pages. There are just symbols at first, then written prayers, some of which seem kind of familiar. I pause to read some out loud to myself before continuing to flip through the notebook. After several more pages, I notice that the handwriting changes and a new entry begins with the name "Lisette Auberjean." This writer had described herself as the caregiver of the household and as someone who had loved someone named Miss Prudence like a mother. She had also written that she felt they were both in danger and prayed to God and to her voodoo queen for help and protection.

I sit up straight in my chair. I cannot believe what I am reading. *Who is Miss Prudence?* I ask myself. I search for the cross amongst the desk's items and put it over my head, letting the heavy weight of it hang around my neck. I don't know why I'm doing it, though. I just feel compelled. As I read on, I feel so sad for this Lisette woman who had seemed very religious and very afraid for herself and Miss Prudence, who I think must have been the woman of the house.

I come across another entry, this one dated August 20, 1849:

May this house and all who reside on its foundation be safe from darkness. May your peace be protected around and within. May purest of hearts have good fortune from your beginning until your end and be guided to the light away from sin.

Toast to good spirits in welcome.

Something in that paragraph makes me feel very warm and comforted. I gaze at the sealed bottle before me and stand up to look for a cup. I break the seal on the bottle of absinthe and inhale. It smells exactly like the powerful spirit Jack had served to me. I pour a little in the paper cup I've found and hold it up to my house, toasting us both. And I drink it down.

CHAPTER THREE

I wake the next morning with my head on my computer desk. I am a little foggy and confused. *Why am I here and not in my bed?* My neck is stiff and my lower back throbs in pain. "What the hell?" I say out loud. I glance around; everything seems normal. The sun is up, brightening the whole room, and I look at the clock. Eleven a.m., Saturday. "Oh, man, I slept way too long…" My eyes dart up to my screen. *What is all this?* I move the mouse up and down, scanning across the characters, then I begin to read. First, I wonder if it is something I left open about the house. Then, I read, and read some more. I realize I am the one who apparently tapped on the computer keys and wrote these paragraphs, but I don't remember doing it at all…

My name is Prudence Henriod Ravensdale. I was born in France in 1777. I came to America in 1798. I had to leave to save myself from the danger that had darkened my sister's life and mine. When I arrived here, I was just twenty-one years of age. I didn't bring much with me. Only the money given to me as payment from an evil man named Marcellis Dubied. He had wanted the recipe for the elixir we made to help heal the sick. It was our secret, and we did not want to divulge our recipe to him or any other. Only the purest of hearts and family bloodline can understand it. He threatened to reveal us as witches. I am a healer, but many fear what they do not understand. Monsieur Dubied even murdered our friend, a doctor, to frighten us, to get us to sell him our recipe…Oh, how I miss our friend, Dr. Ordinaire.

My sister, Jonet, was forced into a marriage to the nephew of M. Dubied. After I fled my homeland, I was never to see my sister again. M. Dubied had wanted us to use our gifts for profit by marketing our healing elixir, but we never gave him the proper recipe. In the end, we were forced out of fear to sell it to him, but we had ommitted a particular healing herb. M. Dubied, some time later, discovered our deception. In the meantime, he had partnered with a winemaker, Louis Pernod. Together, they opened distilleries to produce the elixir, even though it was without the secret ingredient, and named it absinthe. The green liquid became popular, even more so than any of the fine wines in France. As a result, Dubied and Pernod made their fortunes from my family's treasured recipe.

Some years after my arrival in America, I met a wonderful Englishman by the name of Bernard Ravensdale. Soon after our marriage, he moved me south to New Orleans so I could be close to people who spoke my native tongue. We built this house and were blessed with three healthy children. Life became even better when I found Lisette. Half Haitian, half French, she knew many of the healing ways, as I did. Her grandmother, a very strong voodoo queen around these parts, had taught her well. I took her in as an au pair, and together we made our healing powders and elixirs. She went to church with us and cared for my children as if they were her own. Because she was pure light of heart, I shared my family's secret recipe with Lisette, and she was able to make our special green elixir as well as I could.

Much too soon, the darkness of my past followed me here and loomed around us, threatening once again…

I realize I am sitting so still, almost frozen in my chair but taking deep breaths. I don't know how long it took to write those short, completely unfamiliar paragraphs, or how long I was knocked out, or how the words appeared here. But here it sits, all lit up on my computer. *Did I do this? Did Prudence write this? How?*

I search online for the next several hours, trying to find any information at all about the people mentioned in the mysterious writing. Some of the names come up, but there is not much on the Henriod sisters. It would seem that recorded history scrambled it up. I decide that the next thing on my list today will be to go to City Hall to gather information about the house itself. Then, I'll try to contact any living descendants to see what other information I can get.

After a hot shower and some strong coffee, I go to sit out in my garden courtyard, trying to wrap my head around what happened last night. I remember going through the box and the notebook, then the toast I made to the house… "I drank the Absinthe!" I say very loud to no one but the flowers and trees that are scattered across my back yard. "No way…" I shake my head. "Could it have…?" I remember Jack's story about this stuff causing hallucinations. *Holy shit!* I freak out for a minute or two, then I quickly try to calm down. I realize I feel fine—more than fine, actually. But, along with that feeling of wellness, I am somehow picking up an emotion of desperation and an odd sense that my help is needed by Prudence Ravensdale.

I get in my car and head out to City Hall. During the entire drive over there, I am on my cell phone with Helen, the realtor who sold me the house. The first words out of her mouth when I ask her some questions are, "Oh, shit! Please don't tell me the house is haunted!"

"No, no, no…not at all!" I assure her. "I just want to research the history of the house. I found some things behind a wall removed during some renovations." I couldn't tell her that maybe I was the one being haunted in some mysterious way. I wanted information, and I couldn't sound like a complete freak.

"Oh, whew!" She laughs. "Let me see what I can retrieve for you, and I'll get back to you ASAP!"

I thank her and pull into the parking lot. I enter City Hall and ask where the hall of records would be. The clerk shows me to the correct area, and I immediately get to work. I am thrilled to find several pieces of information.

I find out my house was built in 1803 for Mr. and Mrs. B. Ravensdale.

By 1810, there were 3 children, all girls, born to the Ravensdales: Suzette, Juliette, and Andrea.

Mr. Ravensdale was a businessman who came from England. But, here the trail runs cold; there is nothing else. I look up death records, next:

Mrs. Prudence Ravensdale:

Born the 23rd day of October 1777 in Pontarlier, France. Deceased the 10th day of November 1821 at 44 years of age; cause of death unknown. Survived by husband and three children.

"Death unknown? And where did you all go?" I whisper. I continue to look up anything I can about any Ravensdales in the area, but I find nothing more of consequence. Just a quick blurb in a local paper of the time. It stated that Prudence's eldest daughter, Suzette, had gone to the University of Cambridge in England. Upon seeing this, I wonder if the whole family started over after their mother died. Maybe their father took them back to his home because he had lost his wife.

I am deep in thought when the vibration of my cell phone startles me. I reach into the pocket of my jeans and pull out my cell. I'm happy to see it is Helen.

"Hello, Helen. I'm in the hall of records right now, and I found some stuff, but not much. The trail seems to just go cold after Mrs. Ravensdale's death."

"Yes, I didn't find much myself, either, so I made a phone call to a Sebastian Charles Devonshire. His name is the one we have on documents for your house. He is from the U.K. but has dual citizenship. He travels back and forth for business. I had to leave a message with his secretary, so I left your name and number. I hope that was all right?"

"Yes, that's fine. Thank you, Helen. I hope this Sebastian can help me out. He sounds important." I chuckle. "What type of business is he in?"

"I believe he is some kind of CEO or something like that," she replies.

The first thing that comes to my mind is that Mr. Devonshire is probably too busy to talk with me and I might have to get pushy, but I don't care. I need to know the history of my house and of the Ravensdales. I also feel the pull of creativity beckoning. I am obviously sitting on my next book, one that is being told to me, I'm beginning to believe, by what must be the spirit of Prudence Ravensdale. But, what I don't know is why, and I'm still wrapping my head around the how. Before I can even try to write her story, I need more facts. I have too many loose ends. I arrive home exhausted, my mind racing in too many directions and suffering from sleeping at my computer desk all night. I need a nap. I plop down on my sofa and drift into a sound sleep.

***

Across the country, Sebastian C. Devonshire is in a board meeting in his company's New York City office. At thirty-eight, he has already been the head of his family's business for a few years. When his father died, Sebastian had inherited big shoes to fill, but the leadership transition had gone smoothly. With today's meeting finally over, he gathers his things, strides from the office building, and climbs into his waiting limo. As he leans into the comfortable leather seat, his secretary phones to inform him that a Sharie Donovan, who bought the family manor in Louisiana, desperately wants to speak with him.

"I wonder what she could possibly want?"

"Well, sir, she apparently wants some information on the house. It seems there were some items found."

"Items? What kind of items?"

"I'm not sure. All I was told is that she is a writer and wants to know more about the house and its history."

"All right. Thank you, Janice. Please give me her contact information, and I'll try to reach her directly."

"Yes, sir. I'll get that to you right away."

His curiosity aroused, Sebastian googles Sharie Donovan after pouring himself a martini and settling in for the evening at his Fifth Avenue penthouse. "Well, what do have here, Ms. Donavan? Romance and mysteries are your passions, are they?" He sips the martini, the smooth liquor warming his throat. Sharie's big, brown eyes, sincere and friendly, gaze back at him from one of the photos Sebastian happens across. Reading her bio, he detects a sense of humor and adventure. With some free time coming soon, he thinks about taking a trip down south, playing a few rounds of golf, maybe going fishing and paying Miss Donavan a visit. He realizes he hasn't been to the manor since he was a small boy. His mother is the one who stopped wanting to vacation there; she just wanted to be rid of the place. *We haven't been since Father passed,* he remembers. He relaxes back into his leather chair and proceeds to make travel arrangements on the phone. He then emails Miss Donovan:

From: Sebastian C. Devonshire

To: Sharie Donovan

Dear Miss Donovan,

I hope this email finds you well and you are enjoying your new home. I received a message that you are inquiring about the manor and its history. I understand there were some items found. If you would be so kind as to share with me what it is you found and what information you seek, I will do my best to answer your questions.

Sincerely,

S.C. Devonshire

CHAPTER FOUR

I hear my sister's car pull into my driveway. I've told her I would watch Jaqueline while she runs to the restaurant supply store. I get to the door and open it just in time for my niece to run in with Friedo trailing behind her.

"Hi, Auntie Shree!" she yells as she and her four-legged buddy go past me at full speed.

"Hi there, kiddo!" I sing back and wave as my sister makes her way in the door after them.

"Thanks for watching her for a few hours," she says. "I shouldn't be long, but if I am, Jack will call you. He'll come pick her up."

"It's all good." I smile at her. "Don't worry, she has the Cartoon Network and I have some research and writing to get lost in. I'll break for lunch, maybe take them to the park. There is also a spring fair up at the church. I can take her there, if it's okay with you. I promise not to give her too much junk—I remember what happened last time...sorry..."

"Yes, be careful. I never saw so much vomit come out of one little girl in my life!" Charlotte makes a face and shudders. "You have got to learn to say no. She'll get over it." Charlotte turns and shouts towards the T.V. "Jaqueline, I'm going now, and you listen to Aunt Sharie and be a good girl."

"Yes, momma!" she squeals from the living room sofa, already glued to the T.V.

"Go, already." I say with a smile and shoo her away from the door. "I'll see you later."

"Thanks, sis. Charlie is with Jack at baseball practice. I'll have my cell on in case you need me."

"I won't need you; take your time," I say, still trying to shoo her out. I watch her get in her car. I wave one last time then close my door and lock it.

I walk past my niece, glad to see she's snuggled up in a blanket and already involved with cartoons. "I'm going downstairs to my office to work for a while, but if you need me just yell or come down, okay?" Jacqueline nods.

I grab a cup of coffee and head down the few steps to my office. I notice Friedo sitting up on his hind legs begging, or looking at something, on the wall next to my desk. His tail is wagging, and he is whining. "What's up, Friedo? Hey, boy, whatcha got?" He lets out a soft bark, trots over to me in a circle, then goes back to the wall and stares, mesmerized by something there. I approach, ready to squash a bug of some kind, but I don't see anything. I follow the pup's eyes to the area he is concerned with, but nothing is there. "Okay, Friedo, that's enough. Come here, boy." With my soft command, he jumps into my arms and licks my face. I sit down with him on my lap and move my computer mouse to get things started.

As I open my email, I spot something from Sebastian Devonshire. I read it quickly, so surprised and thrilled that he reached out. I hastily write him back, explaining what I've found and asking whether he knows anything about it or has ever found anything like this in the house before. I hit send.

I navigate next to a file where I keep some notes on book ideas. I start to outline a story for my new book. Friedo jumps from my lap and back to the wall. He whines and wags his tail. "Okay, dog," I moan. "Enough. Go upstairs with Jaqueline…Go on!" I tell him. "I have work to do." I clap my hands and he scurries up the steps.

***

A limo waits for Sebastian at the New Orleans airport to drive him to the high-rise penthouse suite he owns on the gulf. A car—either a limo or one of his own—is always ready for him whenever he needs one. The suite has a small staff to do the cooking and cleaning, and they have everything ready at a moment's notice. When he arrives, Sebastion quickly showers and gets dressed, choosing jeans and a white oxford shirt. While still towel-drying his brown, curly hair, he pads over to his computer to check his email and the day's events before heading out for a drink with a few colleagues. His eyes quickly notice the email from Sharie. As he reads it, he feels warm, delighted, maybe even excited that she has answered, and he doesn't quite understand why, but something about this woman is so very intriguing to him. He mentally chides himself. He doesn't even know Sharie Donovan, mystery-romance novelist, for heaven's sake. He raises an eyebrow at the computer screen and sends a brief reply:

Ms. Donovan—

I happen to be in New Orleans, unexpectedly. Shall we meet? What time and day would be convenient for you? Although I have not been to the manor for many years, I'm sure I'll have no trouble finding my way.

Sebastian.

***

As I tap away on my computer, typing notes for my new story, a new email alert pops up on my screen. I'm surprised to see it is another message from Mr. Devonshire. "Well, what do you know?" I say aloud to myself. "I thought he would be too busy to get back to me so soon!" His email makes me a bit giddy, though I'm not sure why. His latest email seems to have a flirty feel to it. I smile widely when I read that he is in town, and I promptly send him my cell phone number with a "call me" reply. I shake my head; I can't believe I just did that! He's basically a stranger. But, I suppose we are going to eventually meet anyway, so why not now?

A few hours into my work, I hear Jaqueline giggling. I turn quickly. She's standing there beside me with her little chubby-cheeked smile, waving her tiny fingers at me.

"Jaqueline, what in the world are you doing?" I tap my chest. "You startled me! What are you giggling at?" Friedo runs down the stairs, jumps onto my lap, and barks and whines at the wall again. Tail wagging wildly, the pup makes my niece giggle even more! "Okay, you two, upstairs. I need more coffee, and I'll make you both some lunch."

My niece looks up at me with her little blue gaze and takes my hand. "Auntie Shree, when you're done working with dat lady can you take me and Fweedo to the fair? Pwitty pleeeaze?"

"Yes, sweetie, we can go to the fair..." Confused, I suddenly realize what else she said. "Jaqueline—what lady?"

***

As I watch Jaqueline munch on her sandwich, I grip a warm mug of coffee tightly with both hands and take a deep breath. "Tell me again, sweetie, so I understand. You saw a lady in my office?"

"Yes," she answers.

"Tell me slowly what she looks like, and—think now, Jaqueline—tell me every little bit about her you can remember, like, is she tall or short? Fat or skinny?"

"She's tall and skinny," she says around her grilled cheese sandwich. Her voice is low and calm. I'm sure she senses that I am a little unnerved, but she doesn't seem afraid of the woman in my office. "She has dark hair pulled up with curls, and a long, dark dress that goes down to the floor. She likes Fweedo, and she has a pwitty smile."

"Okay. Good, sweetie. Now, what exactly was she doing?"

"You're silly, Auntie Shree!" Jacqueline giggles. "You know what she was doing. She was just standing right behind you, watching you write." Obviously, it hasn't even occurred to my niece that I could not see the lady like she could. "Oh," Jacqueline continues, "she points to a necklace on her chest, like this." She puts her little hand right below her collar bone, pointing, then places both hands over one another and presses her chest. "It's like she's pwaying. Aunt Shree, didn't you see her?" Jacqueline asks at last as I stare at her with what must be an odd, blank look.

"No, I didn't," I almost whisper. "Will you do me a favor, though, and let's not tell your mom about this, because it might worry her a little bit. Can you and I have this little secret together? Please?"

"K, Aunt Shree. I won't tell." She crosses her heart with a finger. Then, she ponders for a moment and whispers, "Is she a ghost, Aunt Shree? Because, I'm not a-scared of her. She's fwendly, but…she's sad."

I blew out a deep breath that I didn't realize I was holding and brought my niece up to sit on my lap. "Yeah, sweetie, I think she is, and I think she wants my help." I make her look in my eyes. "Now, I am really going to need your help, but in secret, okay?" I gaze into her cornflower baby blues, and we pinky-swear the deal.

***

After I clean up the lunch dishes, I tell Jaqueline we will go to the parish fair. I am upstairs getting ready when the doorbell rings. I yell for Jaqueline *not* to get the door, but I am too late—I hear a man asking for me.

"Aunt Shree!" My niece's voice pierces through the house. "Someone is here for you!" I race down the steps and find Jaqueline standing in the doorway with a very handsome guy kneeling before her.

"What did I tell you about answering the door, young lady? You know better," I scold. The handsome guy stands to his feet.

"Hello, Ms. Donovan. It's a pleasure to finally meet you." He put out his hand. "I'm Sebastian Devonshire."

"Oh…OH! Hello!" *Holy crap, he's hot.* "Come in, please. I'm so sorry about that. My niece, Jaqueline, should know better than to answer the door if she doesn't know who is there. Please come and sit down."

"Ah, yes. That is a very good rule." Sebastian turns back to her. "Well, hello, Miss Jaqueline. It is such a pleasure to meet you. How old are you?"

"Five." She holds up one hand.

33

"Oh, and how pretty you and your aunt look. Did I catch you both at a bad time? My apologies. Perhaps I should have called first?"

Before I can speak, my niece cuts me off and carries the conversation.

"Aunt Shree is taking me to the fair! Do you like fairs? Maybe you can come. Why do you talk funny?"

"Okay, Jaqueline. Sweetie, slow down. Mr. Devonshire is from England so he has a little accent, and I am sure he doesn't want to go to some fair with us. He is a busy man."

"Please call me Sebastian."

Jaqueline looks up at him. "Nice to meet you, too, S'bass-ten."

"Sebastian." I correct her.

She tried again. "Bash."

"Yes." He looks at us both. "Bash it is, young lady. I rather fancy that. Has a good tone to it." He smiles, and I notice his little five-o'clock shadow and mussed-up, curly, dark hair. His eyes are dark blue, almost navy. He is extremely handsome. I feel myself smile and blush.

"Now, what's this about a fair?" he asks playfully.

I clear my throat. "There's a fair up at the church not far from here. I promised Jaqueline I would take her this afternoon, but I can take her tomorrow…"

"No, no. I would love to go to a fair, but only if it's okay with Jaqueline." She grins and nods her head. "Shall we, then?" He points to the door.

"Are you sure you want to go? We can meet later, or I can take her tomorrow. Really. It's not a big deal..."

"You made a promise to your niece, and I really should have called to tell you I was in the area, but since Jaqueline was so kind to invite me, how can I refuse? Ladies...after you..."

I grab Jaqueline's car seat and we walk out of the house. In my driveway, there sits a late-model Mercedes SUV. My poor little engine that could seems to be sighing in its presence. "I'll drive," he offers. "Everyone in."

"You really don't have to do this. We can meet afterward. Anytime is fine..." I stammer.

"Ms. Donovan, it would be a most welcome pleasure to take two pretty ladies out for some fun and relaxation. I am usually in meetings or behind a computer all day, so really, I would like nothing more than to accompany you both. Now, stop being, as you Americans say...a...*buzz kill*, isn't it?"

I pick my chin up off the ground and laugh out loud. "You got it!" I put my hands up. "Far be it from me to kill anyone's buzz, and please call me Sharie, like Marie but with a *shh*."

"Certainly, Sharie," he says with a long gaze into my eyes. "Now, just point me in the direction of this fair."

So, before I can talk myself out of it, I buckle Jacqueline into the back seat. Then, I hop into the front passenger seat as Sebastian holds the car door open for me and waits to make sure I'm settled before closing my door. He walks around the car and takes his place behind the wheel.

The church isn't far, and as luck would have it, the fair is not too crowded, today. The weather is beautiful—not a cloud in the sky, not too warm or cold. Sebastian appears to be the perfect gentleman and purchases all our refreshments as well as tickets for the attractions. We chat here and there, giggling and flirting as we watch Jaqueline go on the rides. *This feels like a date*, I think to myself, *and I am having a hell of a good time.*

CHAPTER FIVE

Sebastian pulls into my driveway and turns off the car. He is not only being patient and attentive as Jaqueline talks his ear off, but he actually seems to be having fun with her, too.

"That's enough, Jaqueline," I say with a laugh. "We're home, and your mother will be here very soon."

Sebastian comes around the car to open my door and then Jacqueline's. He walks us to the front door, but then I turn swiftly and almost bang my head to Sebastian's nose. "Oh, sorry!" I chuckle. "I just wanted to ask if you would like to come in. I can make us some coffee? Or, tea? Or, maybe you'd like a beer?"

"Sounds lovely, Sharie. Thank you. I think I'll have the beer, and I would love to see what you have done with the old place."

A few minutes after Sebastian and I have settled in with our beers and Jacqueline opts for a glass of juice, my sister Charlotte shows up. I introduce her and Sebastian to each other, and we make awkward small talk. Soon, she gathers up Jaqueline to leave. I walk them to the front door, leaving Sebastian drinking his beer in the kitchen.

"Oh sweet Jesus, Sharie. He's so handsome, it's like he just stepped out of GQ!" Charlotte whispers. "Is he single? What's his deal? And the accent, Sharie…oooh, the accent! That's kind of hot."

"Charlotte! Stop! I know. Stop babbling like a drunk teenager! You sound a lot like your daughter. She talked his ear off all afternoon. I think the kid is smitten with Mr. Devonshire."

"*Fancies* him, I think the English say. And, I believe he fancies you. I can't believe he went with you guys to the fair!"

"Yes, and he paid for everything. Such a gentleman. I guess I kind of fancy him, too," I giggle. "I would like some alone time with him now, so move it out, sister. I'll call you in the morning."

"Okay, okay, but don't forget—I want details!"

"Goodbye, Charlotte."

I stride back to the kitchen and take two more beers from the fridge and pass one to Sebastian. "Would you like another beer? You certainly deserve it after spending the day with my niece and being so tolerant."

"Oh, no worries. She's a cute kid. I can see how much she adores you."

"Yes, since I am the aunt, I get to spoil them and then send them back."

He furrows his eyebrows. "Them?"

38

"Yeah, I have a nephew, too. Jaqueline's older brother, Charlie. He was with his dad, today."

He takes a long pull from his beer. "So, you're just an aunt? No kids of your own?"

"Nope, never been married. It's just me. How about you? What's your story, Mr. Devonshire." I heard my voice drip with flirtation as I spoke.

"I am single at the moment, and I don't have any children. And please do call me Bash—I insist. Now that I'm running my father's company, it's sometimes difficult to have a solid relationship when I travel so much. London...New York. I can be gone for weeks at a time. Women don't usually care for their man not being around much, as I have found out with the last two relationships I've had. "

"They didn't like the long-distance thing, huh?" I ask.

"Let's just say one woman became...quite bitchy, to put it plainly, and the last didn't mind the distance because, as I discovered, she was shacking up with one of my competitors. Good thing I don't kiss and tell secrets, so to speak, amongst business associates."

"Ouch!" I say sympathetically, but then I quickly take a sip of my beer to hide my sly smile at the fact that he is single. "And, what about Louisiana?" I question.

"Well, this old house has been in our family for generations. My grandfather, my mother's father, used to bring the family here every summer from the end of May through the end of August. After he died, it was given to my mother. She hardly ever came here, though, and even less after my father died. She just wanted nothing to do with it;

she told me to sell it. My mother barely leaves England, now, at all."

I study his navy-blue eyes as a boyish smile appears on his face. "What's the matter? You look embarrassed." I smile reassuringly at him.

"It's nothing," he chuckles. "I've only just met you, and yet I've told you some very private things about myself, and I don't know why. I suppose I feel…comfortable around you. So, tell me about yourself, Sharie. I looked you up and read reviews on some of the books you've authored. Very nice. Did you always want to be a writer?"

I finish off my beer and stand up, pointing to the fridge. "Another?" I ask.

"If you are, then I will," he replies.

I grab two more Coors Lights out of the fridge, feeling sorry that I don't have anything more exotic to offer him. "Follow me. You can see the changes I've made downstairs while we chat."

"I haven't been here since I was a young boy, maybe twelve, but I like what you've done here," Sebastian compliments as he surveys my office.

"Thanks," I answer as I offer him a seat and choose a comfortable spot for myself. "So. My turn, huh? Let's see…I dabbled in a few jobs, but I always wrote. For some reason, I felt like it was my dirty little secret. My dad found some things I had written when I was about twenty-three and told me I should do something with my writing, even if it didn't make me wealthy, because it's something I enjoy. Dad used to say, 'If you're doing something you love, then in your heart you're wealthy.'"

"He sounds very wise."

"He was. He died a few years ago. Mom just passed recently. My sister, Charlotte, who you met earlier, and her husband urged me to move here so we could be together, a family. I used to travel a lot to do research for my books."

"I'm so sorry," he cut in. "My condolences on your losses."

"Thank you. It is difficult to lose both your parents, and I certainly miss them. But, hey, it all brought me to this fabulous house—which brings me to this." I walk over to the hutch and the box containing the voodoo artifacts. I set the box on the coffee table in front of Sebastian. "These are the things that were found when my builders removed a wall down here during the renovations." Sebastian looks at the odd contents of the box. "I have been reading some of the material in this notebook, but I think now it's more of a diary. Do you know anything about your ancestors? Anything at all would help me. I have a story simmering in my head, and I feel like I am missing some pieces of a mysterious puzzle." I keep my query a little vague, not wanting to tell him what's really going on. I can just picture this debonair man thinking I am absolutely nuts and running from my house like he's on fire if I were to tell him his ancestor had chosen me from beyond the grave to be her communicator and was doing some ghost writing on my computer while I slept.

"So, you're saying you'd like to write a book about my ancestors? That's fascinating."

"Well, I would say it would be more of a work of fiction," I lie. "You know, build a story around what I've found."

"Oh yes, I understand. Well, to be honest, I don't know much. Just that the house was Grandfather's and willed to him by his mother. But that's all I know. I could ask my mother if she knows anything that could be of help."

"That would be great. I did some snooping on my own, and I know when the house was built and for whom. It was a family with the name Ravensdale. Prudence and Bernard Ravensdale. Are you familiar with those names?"

Sebastian is picking through the box and flipping pages of the notebook. He looks thoughtful for a moment then nods his head in recognition. "Yes, I have heard that name. Prudence was my great-great-great-grandmother on my mother's side, I seem to recall. She was a Henriod from Paris, and she came to the States, married Bernard Ravensdale. They had three girls. I believe I am a descendant of Andrea, her youngest child."

"So, the children lived on after her death!" I shout in surprise.

"Well, yes...'" Sebastian looks at me, confused.

"I looked them up in the hall of records. I found that Prudence had three daughters and that she died rather young, but that's it. The record listed her cause of death as unknown. The trail just goes cold, at that point. I assumed that Bernard took their daughters back to England to be near his family."

"You are correct, but I don't know much more than that, myself. As I said, my mother might have more information, but sadly, there is no one else left to give us any more details, as far as I know."

"Okay," I answer, happy that at least my assumption had been confirmed. "I'm sorry to trouble you with it, but would you mind asking your mother if she could remember anything else about the Ravensdales?" I sit beside him on the tiny love seat in front of the box. He is still looking through all the stuff. Everything is there except the bottle of absinthe. I hid that days ago in my desk drawer. I feel like an alcoholic not wanting to share this, inexplicably wanting to keep it as my secret for now.

"I would be happy to ask her. I hope she can come up with something to help you craft your tale. So tell me, Sharie, have you written anything so far about this?"

I ponder for a moment or two before answering curtly. "Yes and no. It's still in notes, more or less. Like I said, there are pieces missing, but I'll make it work. I usually do."

He takes another long pull of his beer and places it on the table. "I have no doubt you will." He pauses and holds my gaze for a moment. "I read one of your books on the flight over the other day."

"You did? Which one?"

"*In Too Deep*. That was certainly a twisty, sexy mystery, and your facts were spot on. Bravo, Ms. Donovan. With that writing, it's hard to believe you're single."

"Why? You think that writing romance makes the guys line up at my door? On the contrary; it brings the porno freaks out who try to friend me on every social media outlet there is. I try to keep to myself. It drives my publisher crazy. She thinks the books would sell better if I was out more in the public. But, to be honest, that's out of my comfort zone."

He gazes at me with a half a smile playing on his lips. I know this look. My sister may be right—I think he fancies me, or who he thinks I am.

"I should be going," he says. "Thank you for a lovely day." I smile warmly, and he continues, "May I ask, would you care to go to dinner with me this Saturday night? I would thoroughly enjoy your company again, Ms. Donovan."

I stand; he follows. "I would like that very much." We stare at each other for a second. "My sister and her husband own a fantastic restaurant not too far from here. It's called Rendezvous. Have you heard of it?"

"Why yes, I believe I have. I shall make reservations there for Saturday at seven, if you'd like."

"Seven would be fine. My sister is the chef; she's really talented."

We walk back upstairs and over to the front door. We stand there for another awkward moment, but then he reaches for my hand. "Good night, Sharie. Until Saturday."

He looks delicious. In my head, I'm screaming for him to kiss me. Then, as if reading my mind, he leans closer and says softly, "Sharie, I hope I'm not being too forward, but I must…"

His kiss is sweet and hot, his hands grip my waist, holding me still while our tongues twirl together. I feel my knees go a little weak. It's been far too long since I have been kissed like this. His hands move up my ribs, around my shoulders to my neck, and then he gently has my face, his fingers sliding through my hair, giving me a chill. He holds my head steady but gently so as not to break our kiss. Finally, we come up for air.

"Yes, that was nice," he says with a smile. "You intrigue me so, Ms. Donovan. I couldn't help myself. I'll see you Saturday night."

He leaves me at the door. I can barely stand. I feel my breathing slow down to normal as he climbs into his car and drives off. I close and lock the door, leaning my head against the cool wood. *Dear God, help me.*

***

Sebastian drives full force all the way back to his place, realizing he has a stupid grin on his face. *What has this woman done to make me stumble over my words? I feel so foolish.* He thinks about her big, amber-brown eyes. They had reminded him of the soft eyes of a doe. Her silky hair and creamy, fair skin…and those lips. Oh God, he couldn't resist kissing her, her lips were that luscious. Her body had felt way too good in his hands, and the more he thinks of it all, and the kiss, the more excited he gets. *Bloody hell, I'm going to need a cold shower before bed.*

CHAPTER SIX

When I can finally think straight, I take a deep breath and glance at the wall clock to check the time. It's not too late, and there is no way I am going to sleep now, anyway. I decide to go to my office and turn on my computer. I open the files containing my notes on the Ravensdales.

I figure I can work for a while, but when I try to concentrate, all I can think about is what a fucked-up day I've had. First, my niece and her dog can see the spirit of Prudence Ravensdale, who somehow is channeled through me when I sip the green elixir. Then, we spend a day with the most charming and handsome man I've ever laid my eyes on, who is related to the spirit, and who gave me a kiss that heated me to my core. *Seriously*, I think, *I couldn't make this shit up if I tried!*

Reading through my notes, I remember what Jaqueline had told me: *"She's pointing to a necklace."*

"Necklace?" I whisper, echoing my thought. I go to the box and pull out the necklace with the cross and roses. I wonder if it was this that Jacqueline saw. I flip through more pages of the notebook, but there is nothing other than some sketches that appear to be of a landscape, a tree or bush, and a path; along with what might be more prayers, or maybe spells; but nothing that helps or frightens me. "Why can't I see you, Prudence?" I call out into an empty room. "Come on, I'm right here!"

Nothing...

I stare at my desk drawer. "Oh, hell. Why not?" I reach for the bottle of absinthe and take a good swig. It stings, and the bitter but unique flavor flows past my taste buds down my throat, coating my stomach with an almost soothing heat. It's not so harsh this time. I feel more warm and fuzzy. Not like before when it felt like a hole being burned into my gut. The liquid is comforting me like an old friend or a favorite blanket.

***

Without warning, men came. Marcellis Dubied had hired them to seek me out. First, they asked nicely for the remaining ingredient for my special elixir. Both Bernard and I told them that M. Dubied has the whole recipe. There is nothing more to tell. Dubied's men informed me that my sister, Jonet, had gone mad and leapt from a high window to her death.

I didn't believe them, of course. I know they must have killed her. I also believe her husband, who did not love her, was probably the master of the whole plan. Money and power drove the Dubied family, and they abused their power by controlling anyone who would not cooperate.

They left us but said they would return. Within these days, Lisette and I created more elixir. I told her to take the bottles and hide them away and never divulge our secret herb. For it was not for everyone to know. In the wrong hands, this would be too powerful and could even be deadly.

We prayed together and hoped for the best. After a few weeks had passed, it was all too quiet. One night while we were having our meal, a rock came crashing through a window with a note that read: "Leave, witch!" It frightened me so! My husband ran to the door, but no one was there. I sent the girls to bed and told them to stay together and lock themselves in for the night.

The next day, the men returned to tell us it would get worse from here if I did not comply with their demands. If I did, however, they assured me the brutality would end. I told them nothing, for I knew from this moment on, whether I told them or not, they were going to kill us.

The next night, rotten apples and rocks pelted the house, while in the daylight hours the people in my own parish were turning their backs on us, calling us witches. I knew the cruelty had gone on for far too long when Juliette came home with her baby sister Andrea covered in bruises and blood from stones being thrown at them by the other children, and Juliette's face showed a gash above her eye. Bernard loaded his guns and told me he was going to kill anyone who set foot on our property. But I knew we would not survive this, at least not all of us.

I gave Bernard an option; my dear husband was so torn. I told him I would die for my children and for him, as this was not their fault or their fight. "Pack up the girls and go far away," I told him. Lisette would help me from then on. I assured him that, once the danger was passed, if I survived, I would go to be with him and the children in England. If not, they would all still have been kept safe from the evil that had fallen upon us.

Finally, Bernard reluctantly agreed to take the girls to England and wait for me there…

***

When I awake at my keyboard, it's morning, just like before. I feel a little dizzy…or fuzzy, as if I've been under water. Gradually, it passes. I look up and read the screen. "Oh….my…God!" As I quickly read through the words on my screen, I am beside myself once again. I don't remember typing any of it. "My God, Prudence. What happened?" I speak aloud and glance around the room, but it remains quiet. I am suddenly jerked out of my zone by the ring tone of my cell. It's Charlotte. "Hmm…this should be interesting," I say under my breath.

"Good morning, sister." I yawn into the phone.

"Good morning!" she sings. "Well, anything go down with Bash last night?"

"Bash?" I question her.

"Yes, Jaqueline talked about the 'man named Bash' all night till she fell asleep. I think my daughter has her first crush!"

"Yes, and I can't say I blame her. Bash is very debonair, very gentlemanly, and way out of my league. The man can kiss, though! Holy Jesus, he almost melted my panties, Charlotte!"

"Oh, I knew it! I saw his face, the way he was looking at you—wait a minute. Out of your league? What the hell is that supposed to mean, Sharie?" The scolding tone in her voice sounds just like Mom.

"Come on," I answer. "You know. He's incredibly wealthy. He can have anyone he wants: a supermodel, an actress…Why me? I'm a plain, ordinary nobody. He flies back and forth between here and New York and England all the time. It could never work. But, he did ask me to dinner

Saturday night. He's going to be calling you for reservations."

"First of all, you *are* somebody: you are my beautiful, talented, and very funny sister. I can see why he would want you. You don't give yourself enough credit. All that other stuff you mentioned—well, just wait and see what happens. Sounds to me like you're putting on the brakes before you even take off. Don't sabotage what isn't there, Sharie."

I roll my eyes. "Easy for you to say! He didn't give you a kiss that blew your mind, and he didn't look into your soul with those eyes, dark blue and dreamy. And, I can tell you his body is rock hard; I felt it when we kissed."

"Yep, very dreamy," my sister coos. "I'm thrilled for you, Sharie. Just play it cool. Let up off the brakes and glide. I can tell you're unraveling." She laughs.

"Agreed," I answer. "Listen, I'm gonna go. I need coffee and a shower in the worst way. Then, I need to get some work done. Call you later, sis."

***

Sebastian, eating his breakfast, picks up his cell and sends a call through. To his delight, the person on the other end picks up on the first ring.

"Hello, Mother," he says with a smile. "Are you well?"

"Hello, dear. Yes, I'm fine. Where are you, today, Sebastian? Still in the States?"

"Yes, as a matter of fact, I am. I'm in Louisiana at the penthouse. I took an impromptu trip to speak with the

50

young woman who bought the house. Mother, may I ask you some questions?"

"What is it, Sebastian?" Her voice sounded worried. "Is there something wrong?"

"No, no. Not at all. The woman, Sharie Donovan is her name, found some rather odd things at the house while doing some renovations."

"What kind of things?"

"Well, to be honest, I believe some would identify the items as voodoo paraphernalia—a charm or amulet of some kind, candles, and little bottles of powders. Can you imagine? It's really quite macabre. I'm not sure whether Sharie recognized them as such, and I didn't want to mention it and cause her to worry. Sharie is a writer, Mother, and what she's found has inspired her to begin to write a new story, but she would like to know more about the house as well as our ancestors who owned it. I wonder if there's anything more you could tell me that might assist her in her research?"

"Where did she find these things, Sebastian? Maybe some hooligans broke in and..."

"No," he cut in, "it wasn't like that. She had a wall removed, and the objects were behind it in a desk of some sort. Maybe Grandfather or another relative stuck it back there a long time ago. Tell me, Mother, do you know anything at all about this?"

"I don't know a thing, and what do you mean she's writing a book about it? What kind of a book? Sebastian, listen to me. Just indulge me and don't return to that house. Stay out of it. It's not ours any longer and not our problem.

51

You don't need to give her any further information. I don't like this one bit," she said, her voice starting to tremble.

"Firstly, Mother, calm down. You sound a bit of a fright. Secondly, Sharie writes fiction. You know, mystery-romance novels and all that. Just a bit of fun, really. Look, she's also found a little notebook of some sort there with fanciful writing in it. It's just given her ideas for a book, nothing to get so concerned about. Thirdly, what are you going on about? 'Stay away from the house.' How absurd. Is there something you're not telling me, Mother? Because, if there is, you need to come out with it, right now. I'm not going to lie to you; I have rather taken a fancy to Ms. Donovan. She is quite lovely, I enjoy her company, and I have already asked her to dinner. So, if there is something you need to tell me, you had better do so."

Silence hung in the air for a moment until his mother cleared her throat. "I haven't a thing to tell you about that house. I am just looking out for your well being. Make sure this Sharie isn't hiding something, herself. I am sure by now she knows we are very well off. And, well, you know how certain types of women can be."

He chuckles at her assumption. "I can assure you, Mother, so far I don't think Sharie is hiding anything, and I am the one who initiated the pursuit."

"Of course you did," she said, her voice oozing with sarcasm.

"What can I say? You taught me to be charming and irresistible. Ladies just fall at my feet, Mother." He sighs. "I won't give up till I find some happiness of my own, just as you and dad were fortunate enough to have."

"I know, dear. Just be careful."

"I always am, Mum. No worries," Sebastian assures her.

"Oh, Sebastian—before you go, tell me, did you see what was written in the notebook Miss Donovan found?"

"Uh…yes. It was mostly like prayers, or chants. Some symbols…a few drawings. To be honest, it looked like a bunch of rubbish to me. I couldn't make heads or tails of it. Sharie just wants to spin a fictional tale out of it all, and we were hoping you might be able to shed some light or knew of something interesting she could use. That's all. She has been to the local hall of records and has a bit of background information on the family. I told her we are, in fact, descendants of the Henriod-Ravensdale line, but that's all there is, nothing further. Do you know of any living relative we have who would know anything?"

"No, son, no one is left. I am sorry I can't be of more help to you."

"Right. Okay, then. Well, I must be off. I will chat with you again, soon. Goodbye, Mother."

Ending the conversation, Sebastian senses his mother had not been forthcoming with something, but what? He knew she didn't like to go to the house any more, for whatever reason, and had begged for it to be sold. His mother had sounded more than a little nervous about the whole thing, and he couldn't help but wonder if his own mother was the one hiding something.

***

In the late-afternoon sun, Cornelia Devonshire sits and sips her tea. As a result of the phone conversation with her son, she feels cold all over, and her stomach churns with fear. She was never so happy as when she had learned that awful house had been sold. She had thought she was finally rid of it.

Never in a million years did she think things might be stirred up. She wonders now if the voodoo trinkets were the only things Ms. Donovan had discovered. She wonders in fright if the house could be speaking to Ms. Donovan just as it had to her.

Her great-grandmother had told her there was unfinished business in that house, that her ancestor, Prudence, who was said to have been a healer of the sick, had eventually turned to witchcraft and therefore roams the halls in unrest. Cornelia shudders as she thinks about it. Now, her son might be getting involved in something he'd never imagined. Cornelia whispers a prayer and hopes this is just nothing, but deep down she knows better. She can feel it.

CHAPTER SEVEN

Still sitting at my computer, I try to wrap my head around all the information I have discovered so far, but it seems almost impossible. A story is being told to me from beyond the grave. Prudence and Jonet Henriod had been forced to divulge their family's secret elixir recipe, but they had withheld one key ingredient for which Jonet was murdered and Prudence and her family had been terrorized. The green elixir I found and have been sampling must have been made from the original Henriod recipe containing the missing herb so desperately sought by Dubied.

On the other hand, maybe I have lost my freaking mind. "That's got to be it!" I say under my breath, tossing a pen in the air. Here I am, deciphering a story that I have written while unconscious. Crazy. I think about pulling the bottle out of my desk drawer and having another sip, but I glimpse the clock. I have a date tonight with Mr. Charming. I lose all sense of time when I drink that stuff. Only God knows how long I'm out. "Soon, Prudence," I say to my empty room "I'll put more pieces of this puzzle together and find out what happened to you. Just hang in there."

A few hours and a shower later, my doorbell rings. I check myself in the mirror one last time and think, *This is it. It's not getting any better. It is what it is.* I had gone with the classic little black dress and sexy heels, big sparkly earrings, and a simple, silver chain with a little diamond cross pendant. I open the door, and there he is, wearing a black suit and a white, button-down dress shirt. With a couple of buttons open at the top, I can see just enough chest hair to make my stomach do a flip. His face is clean shaven, his sable-brown hair tousled. The smell of his cologne breezes by me in a mix of spice and leather. He is holding a necktie in his hand.

"Sharie." His voice is smooth.

"Hello, Sebastian. Please come in." I step aside and he strides through the door. He looks me up and down then finds my eyes. A small, bashful smile plays upon his mouth.

"You look magnificent, Sharie. I wasn't sure if I should wear a tie tonight. I wear one most days at the office, and they are so confining. But, if I must…" He holds it up.

"Oh—no, you don't have to wear one," I cut in. "I like this look, and there is no requirement for a tie at Rendezvous. It's pretty laid back and fun. It's a bit early, so we have time for a drink before we go. Would you like something? A glass of wine, maybe?"

"Wine would be perfect, Sharie. Thanks."

He follows me to the kitchen. I grab a bottle of Merlot and the opener. "Oh, here," he says. "Please allow me." I hand him the bottle and then retrieve two glasses from the cabinet and place them on the counter. He pours. "Here's to a wonderful evening, Sharie." We clink our glasses, take a sip, and walk back to the living room, settling ourselves on the sofa.

"I was very much looking forward to seeing you tonight, Sharie. I…uh…rather missed you," he says with a cute smirk. "Tell me, were you able to make any progress on your story, yesterday?"

I let out a breathy laugh. "Okay, I confess. I found it a little tough to concentrate. I kept thinking about what you might have been doing, too. That was some kiss you left me with the other night. Do you always kiss and leave a girl hanging?"

He lets out a laugh. "Yes, I suppose I gave you one of my good ones. As for leaving you hanging, let's see if I can fix that."

He leans in and presses his lips to my mouth, gently at first, then nudging his tongue in and swirling it with mine. Before I realize it, I am on my back and I can feel him harden through his slacks. As he lifts his head to look at me, his mouth a little swollen and pink, I am breathless.

"Forgive me. I just seem to lose control when I'm with you, Sharie. I say we finish our wine and go to dinner, or we may not leave at all." He straightens but keeps his arm curved around my back to pull me gently up with him to a seated position.

I fluff out my hair and giggle. "I suppose I feel the same. I don't even know how I just ended up on my back. Very smooth, Bash," I joke.

He laughs, wipes his mouth, and takes another sip of his wine. "So"—he clears his throat—"you were about to tell me if you'd made any progress on your writing. Please, let's talk about something else so I can get my mind off those beautiful lips of yours."

Smiling, I nod in agreement. "Umm…yes, writing. I did write a few pages, yesterday. I'm weaving a story, but it is still tricky without more information. Did you ask your mother anything? Do you have any interesting material for me?"

"I did talk with Mother, yes. But, unfortunately she had nothing to tell me," he says as he shrugs apologetically. "She…uh…seemed a bit out of sorts about the whole thing. I don't really know what's going on there."

"Oh?" I tilt my head. "Is she all right with me writing a book? It is mostly fiction, of course. Did you tell her about the box of voodoo artifacts?"

He nods, his eyes looking off somewhere far then back to me. "So, you thought the items were voodoo-related, too? I didn't want to mention my suspicions about that the other day, in case you hadn't come to the same conclusion. But, yes, Mother seemed a bit frightened by your discovery. So much so, in fact, that she wanted me to stay completely out of it and never return to this house. I told her she was acting ridiculous. I don't really know what's gotten into her."

"Hmmm…It's a funny thing. These voodoo items seem to make a lot of people uncomfortable. The workmen who tore down the wall wouldn't even touch the things. I'm not picking up a bad vibe at all, but around New Orleans, a lot of people just clam up if they think voodoo is involved. It's tough to get anyone to discuss it."

"Yes, I suppose you're right about that. To me, it's nonsense. Rubbish, really." Sebastian looks at his watch and then back at me. "We should go. I don't want to be late, especially if your sister is cooking us a special meal." He stands and offers me his hand. "Shall we, Ms. Donovan?"

Ignoring his hand, I quickly stand and playfully place my hands on my hips. "What's this about a special meal? Did you talk to my sister?" I glare at him jokingly through squinty eyes.

"As a matter of fact, I did." He grabs me around the waist and lightly gives me a peck. "She said she was going to give us a very nice treat. She sounded thrilled that I asked you to dinner. I hear you don't get out much." He chuckles.

My mouth drops open. "I'm gonna kill her! What did big mouth tell you? I don't believe her…"

He cut me off with a finger to my lips. "Easy, tiger. We had a very lovely chat. Don't be cranky. She is excited to spoil us with a wonderful dinner, so walk those gorgeous legs out to the car so we can get there to enjoy it."

I snap my mouth shut, take a deep breath, and glide out to the car on a cloud.

When we arrive at the restaurant, the place is busy. They have live music tonight, a good, local band that plays a little of everything. The tables are full and the bar is packed. I see Kevin's face light up when he spots us from across the room. He scurries over and gives me a huge hug.

"Hello, gorgeous!" he squeals. "I have a book for you to sign." Then, he leans in to whisper, "So, who's the tall hunk of hotness with you? My God, is he dreamy."

"Kevin, this is Sebastian Devonshire," I introduce them, and they shake hands and exchange pleasantries. Kevin's eyes go wide after hearing the accent, and he blushes.

"Come on, you two," he croons. "I have a special table waiting for you." Kevin shows us the way as Bash gestures for me to go ahead then places his hand at the small of my back as he follows. I glance at Jack, who is behind the bar mixing a cocktail, and he waves. Bash holds my chair for me and pushes me in then takes his seat across from me. Instantly, Kevin returns with a bottle of wine and two glasses.

I look up at him. "What's this?"

He smiles. "With your chef's compliments."

I laugh. "Wow, my sister is not fooling around tonight." Glancing at the wine label, I recognize one of their high-end bottles.

"Your sister is being very generous." Bash smiles. "I told her to give us her best, but I must insist upon paying for it."

"No worries," I say. "My sister likes doing things like this. It makes her happy."

Soon, Kevin returns with his book that I'd promised to sign for him. I write a little personal message, then my name. Kevin gives me a cheesy grin as he thanks me and trots away.

Bash smiles, too. "That must be fun," he says. "Do you sign many books or do many personal appearances?"

"Yes," I answer. "I do enjoy that part of being a writer. It makes me very happy when readers enjoy my stories. I try to do some book signings here and there, but like I said before, I'm not a big fan of being in a spotlight. It's uncomfortable for me."

"I suppose I can understand that. Though, don't you have some fans who would like for you to have a book discussion? Say, in an auditorium-type setting?"

"Yes," I chuckle. "I have done a few, but I do more discussions on line. Again, it's out of my comfort zone."

"Do you consider yourself more of a loner, Sharie? Maybe this is this something I can help you with. In my business, I have to talk with associates from all over the world, sometimes through interpreters. I'm often asked to speak at charity events and colleges, too. Once you've done a dozen or so public speaking events, I believe it won't be such a displeasure for you."

Finally, the first course arrives, and I change the subject. Bash's lips give a slight sideways smile as he seems to realize I really don't like to talk too much about my writing. So, I make small talk about the food then change back to the topic ever present in my mind: the mysteries of my house.

"So, you said you haven't vacationed at the house since you were a boy, right? What do you remember?"

"Not much, really." He picks up his napkin from his lap and wipes his mouth. "Let me see. I must have been, oh, at the very most twelve or thirteen during my last summer there. It used to be such fun, I remember. I loved going into New Orleans; a young chap can get himself into all kinds of mischief there. Some mornings we would go fishing out in the bay, and in the balmy evenings we would just relax. One night in particular, I overheard my parents having a

61

little spat. Mum wanted to leave earlier than scheduled. My father told me she was not feeling well and just wanted to go back to England, so we left almost an entire month early. And that was that. Only Dad came back here when he was on business trips, and he would let other family or friends use it on occasion. We had a crew there all the time keeping the place up—you know, the grounds and whatever maintenance was required in the house itself. But, I had never come back until now, and my mother never wanted to at all. She always said she'd just lost interest in coming here."

"And, after your father died, your mother just wanted to sell?" I question him further. "What were her reasons for getting rid of a house that had been in her family for so long? It must have been for, like, two hundred years!"

He chuckles. "Two hundred and ten, actually. She really never spoke about it. One day, she just told me to sell it. She had absolutely no interest in the house any longer."

"Wow! Well, I guess when my mother got older and after my dad passed, she got really stuck in her ways. It got harder to take her anywhere, like on a vacation or sometimes even a day trip. My mom would go days without leaving the house. Charlotte and I were thinking it was some sort of phobia, but I think this might be something brought on with age."

He nods as he takes another bite of the delectable creation Charlotte has prepared for us. "I might have to agree with you there because, the older my mother gets, the more ill at ease or afraid she seems even over the tiniest things. For instance, about the way she reacted to you writing a book around the manor and the Ravensdales. I told you earlier that she wanted me to stay away from the house, but she wanted me to stay away from you, too." His indigo glare sears through me. "But I told her it was too late. I didn't want to stay away, and we were having dinner together this evening."

I choke on my wine and grab my napkin. "You told your mother about our date?"

He laughs. "Of course. I have nothing to hide. I'm a grown man. My mother has no say about who I date or choose to marry."

I put my napkin down and look up at him. I feel a dumb smile move my lips. Those eyes of his make me weak. "No..." I say softly, "I think it's sweet you told your mother about me. And, by the way, you just gave me a wonderful book title!"

His eyebrows shoot straight up in childlike surprise.

"I did?" he questions. "Come on, then—out with it!"

I smile like the Cheshire cat and say, "Ravensdale Manor."

A smile as slow as molasses spreads across his lips. "Ms. Donovan, that is a brilliant title. Well done!"

Bash pours more wine into our glasses, and we toast—to the book, the title, and the manor.

CHAPTER EIGHT

After dinner, Charlotte comes out of the kitchen and Jack steps away from his post at the bar to sit and have lattes with us. We all get along just fine. Bash compliments my sister on the wonderful meal she prepared for us, all with a New Orleans flair to every dish. After a little conversation, the guys start to talk business and my sister keeps tapping my leg under the table to secretly tell me how much she likes Bash. I glare at her and mouth the word "S-T-O-P." She giggles, and I just shake my head.

"Seriously," I whisper. "How old are you? Cut it out!"

"Oh, you're a kill joy, Sharie. Both of them are clueless as to what we are doing or saying."

"Regardless," I continue, "you're making me nervous, and I have been on edge all night."

"Why? What's up with you, Sharie? I've never seen you act so jittery around a guy before. Is there something going on?"

"No, what could be going on?" *She knows when I'm lying. Hope I'm hiding it well enough.* "I just met him; it's all new. And, yeah...I'm extremely hot for him," I say softly through gritted teeth.

Charlotte breaks out in a blast of giggles. Jack and Bash look across the table at us, wide eyed. "Is everything all right over there, ladies?" Bash asks with amusement in his voice.

"Fine. We are just fine," I answer with a big, dumb smile.

Jack taps Bash on the shoulder. "Hey, maybe I should warn you about these two. Never for a minute underestimate them. They are usually laughing about something I did or something they are gonna get me to do." He points at my sister and me.

"Oh, you're lying!" my sister squeals. "That's not true...is it?" She glances at me.

My smile is smug, and I laugh lightly. "Yeah, it kind of is."

"See. Told you," Jack replies.

We all laugh, and I feel Bash's eyes on me. I'm right in his center of focus. He reaches for my hand right in front of Charlotte and Jack and casually entwines his fingers with mine. "This is great, Sharie. You have a very nice family. You should be very thankful you all have each other. It's lovely." He turns his blue gaze to my sister. "And you, Charlotte, are an amazing chef. Dinner was exceptional. Thank you."

"Any time, Sebastian. It was a pleasure to meet you. We hope to see you again."

"Of that there is no doubt," he says, with a light kiss to the top of my hand. "I can assure you."

Oh shit, this guy is so charismatic he is going to charm the g-string right off me.

He stands up. "Well, we must be off now. I have very much enjoyed our time together, but I would selfishly like to spend the remainder of the evening alone with Sharie, if that would be all right with you?" He smiles in my direction.

I stand up next to him, still connected by our hands. "I would love that." I feel my face flush as a shy smile appears on my lips. We say our good-nights to Charlotte and Jack and head out to the parking lot and into the car.

"Where are we going now?" I ask.

"Oh, I thought we would just go have a little fun. Do you like to play pool, Ms. Donovan?" His voice is playful.

"A little. It's been a while," I say. This may be a good idea. Maybe a beer and low-key atmosphere will calm my jitters, as Charlotte says.

In a few minutes, we pull up to Curly's, the local sports bar. Mostly locals hang here. It's dark, very low key, and there's always something good on the jukebox. The place also has about eight pool tables.

Bash parks the car and helps me out. "Have you ever been here before?" he asks.

"Once or twice with Jack and Charlotte, but it's been a while. You?"

"Yes. Love it," he says. "I like to come here after work to unwind and clear my head. Sometimes after a few rounds of golf, I'd rather come here, too. The country club is a bit stuffy for me. I happen to fancy more of a pub atmosphere."

I smile with relief as we shuffle through the big, wooden door. I'm glad to hear Bash isn't as pretentious as I'd thought.

We find a lonely highboy table, just far enough away from most of the pool tables and the crowded bar. Only two other tables, up front by the jukebox, are occupied by what appear to be some college kids.

I settle onto a bar stool, and Bash leaves me to get us some beers. While I wait, I scope out the nearest pool table, rack up the balls, and choose a cue stick. *Wonder if I should tell him I'm a pretty good shot. Nah...I'll let him figure it out.*

He returns with two frosty mugs. "Coors Light all right?" he asks.

I nod, grabbing the pint from him and taking a sip. "Nice and cold, just the way I like it."

He smiles and points to the table. "All ready to play, I see. Would you like to break first?"

"Oh, all right. Let's see," I say, picking up my stick. Bash centers the triangle of pool balls, lifts the rack gently, and backs away.

I take the chalk and rub it over the end of my stick, place the cue ball in its spot, and place my stick in the ready position. I take a breath…and shoot. The pool balls take off in all directions, sinking into various holes on the table. I stand there, watching where they all end up. "I sank more solids," I say.

Bash is behind me. "Yes, I see that," he says. "I have a fabulous view."

I turn to face him and take the few steps back to the table to grab my mug. "You can see from back here?" I ask, glancing at the pool table.

He nods slyly. "I can see what I need to from here."

I motion for him to go. The cue ball had ended up on the other side of the table. As he is just about ready to take his shot, I make my way over to stand behind and slightly to the side of him. When he bends to take his turn, I see his strong back through the fitted, white dress shirt and the way his ass looks in his trousers—firm and solid. Just as he pulls back the cue stick, I abruptly blurt, "You're right. The view is amazing back here."

He freezes, cue stick in place. "Touché, Ms. Donovan."

He repositions and takes his shot. I glide closer to the table and watch him mentally following the pool balls rolling around on the bluish-green felt. He seems happy with the outcome of his turn. It's good, but not good enough.

"My turn!" I croon, retrieving my pool stick and eyeing up my next shot. He watches me with just the movement of his eyes, a cute slight smile cocking off to one side of his mouth. Still assessing my shot, I notice the cue ball has ended up in a difficult position, but it's nothing I can't handle.

"Would you care for some help making that shot?" he asks. His tone is thoughtful. Before I can answer, he presses up gently behind me at my back and bends me over the table with the slight pressure of his open hand. "See, just keep your back nice and straight. Good," he says. "Keep your feet firmly planted and slightly spread apart," he continues while putting his foot in between mine to push them a little further apart. He bends over me with our bodies together then runs his hand down my back and over my ass. His lips are close to my ear as he whispers, "Perfect. Now, line it up. Eye the shot. Can you feel it?"

I swallow hard and nod. "Then go for it, Sharie. Don't be afraid."

I crack the cue ball, and it sinks the ball into the hole. His hands are firm on my hips as he spins me around, our faces close. "That was a good shot, Ms. Donovan. Maybe a little too good."

"Not my first picnic," I say, gazing into his eyes, where a cobalt brilliance dances like blue fire and makes my breath hitch. He suddenly seals his mouth to mine. The kiss is strong, and my fingers tangle in the back of his hair as he presses me against the pool table. I want to wrap my legs around this man and devour him whole. Finally, as if he remembers we are in a public place, he pulls his mouth from mine. Still holding me in his tight embrace, he sucks in a deep breath and exhales. His eyes burn into mine. "I'd like to get you home now, Sharie." His voice is thick.

"Well," I say on a shaky breath, "what are you just standing there for? You better hurry up."

Bash holds my hand as he drives to the manor. My heart pounds in my chest, and I breathe hard with excitement and anticipation. I know the feeling is mutual as his own strong pulse thumps wildly in our clasped hands and I realize he is driving like a bat out of hell.

We arrive safely, and he reaches for my key to open the front door. Once inside, we lock lips again, our hands finding each other, grasping each other. He scoops me up off my feet and heads for the stairs. He hesitates. "Sharie." He says my name on a breath as if asking for permission. I place my hands on his face. Fiercely I kiss him as if to answer our burning desires.

We enter the bedroom. He places me on my bed, tosses his jacket to the floor, and climbs on top of me. Our kiss is pure heat. Pawing at each other's clothes, he manages to unzip my dress and I unbutton his shirt. He slips my dress down over my shoulders, finding my breasts with his mouth, kissing and licking back up to my neck then down again as he slides my dress over my hips and off.

I reach for the zipper on his pants and feel him hard and ready. He stands to shrug off his pants. He is one magnificent male. He reaches for his jacket pocket, finds his wallet, and pulls out a condom.

I turn off the light. In the darkness, he finds me and I am encircled by his arms. His kiss is soft as he slowly explores my body with his hands. My stomach quivers as he slides a finger through the slickness of my arousal. I dig my fingers into his muscular back as he delves in and out of me, heating my essence. "Now," I tell him. "I want you now."

Arranging himself at my core, he slowly pushes in. He moans my name on a hiss of breath and sinks all the way in. Sebastian moves his hips back and forth. I match his every thrust and feel him inside me, bringing me closer to climax.

When I wrap my legs around his waist, our bodies sleek with sweat, I suddenly feel the orgasm rip through me like a storm. A moan cracks in my throat, and he comes along with me. Our bodies shudder as we hold on to each other, tight. We finally begin to catch our breath between kisses, slowly calming in the aftermath. I feel like I could explode, I am so hot.

Bash cradles me in his arms and scatters feather-light kisses all over me. "Are you all right, luv?" he whispers in the dark.

"I'm fine…more than fine," I chuckle "My God, I could eat you alive. You make me so hot. I almost had an orgasm on the drive home!"

"That goes for us both, luv." He lifts my chin with his finger. "You have five minutes."

"Five minutes?" I question him. "For what?"

"To catch your breath. We are not even close to being done."

***

Bash made love to me almost all night long, and we slept till eleven this morning. I am surprised at the brunch he's managed to cook up for me in my kitchen. After enjoying the meal together, we tidy up the kitchen then stroll from room to room, with Bash commenting that everything looks the same as he remembers aside from some of my redecorating.

We decide to shower and head out, eager to spend more time together. Sebastian takes me first to his high-rise penthouse condo overlooking the Gulf before we venture down to the private pier where a sleek, good-sized yacht is docked.

"This is yours?" I point to the boat that was bigger than an apartment I used to rent.

"She's all mine," he says, smiling. He runs his fingers quickly through his tousled brown locks. "Believe it or not, I won her in a Polo match in England. A business mate of mine, he bought a new one and told me I could have this one, but I had to win it from him."

"So I guess you're good at polo, too?"

He laughs. "Not particularly. Let's just say my friend had some horse problems that day, and the match went in my favor."

"Oh, I see...Do you sail her?"

"Not alone. She has a small crew to run things proper. I have taken her to the Bahamas and up to Bermuda but haven't had a reason to use her, lately. Tell me, luv, do you get seasick?"

"No, I don't. Are we going to take her out?" I ask with excitement.

"Not today. I need more notice for preparation, but I will set something up soon and take you out. It's quiet out there at night. And you can see every star."

"Sounds lovely, Bash. I can't wait."

We stroll along the shoreline, holding hands and stopping every so often to kiss. I tell him more about myself and my adventures traveling and getting ideas for stories.

In the corner of my mind, there is Prudence. I want to tell him so badly about the adventure I am having right now in my own house, the house I've bought from him, the house we've just made passionate love in all night. But, I'm still not sure how he would react to this kind of thing. Some days, I still don't understand it all myself. Jaqueline is my proof, though, that it's not just in my own mind. I decide to wait to see if our relationship becomes more solid before I tell him—or maybe I won't have to tell him at all.

Back inside his penthouse, we sit and eat a lovely dinner, prepared for us by his staff, out on his terrace. We watch the sun sink down into the horizon, sip wine by candlelight and moonlight, and watch the ocean lap at the small crescent-shaped beach in the distance. We kiss with force and purpose until he breaks apart from me, his lips swollen as I can feel mine are, too. He rubs his thumb over mine and smiles slightly.

"I need to get you home, Sharie. Monday mornings are hell for me with work. I am leaving for England on Wednesday. May I see you before then?"

"Bash, you can see me whenever you like," I chuckle. "You know where I am."

His baby blues search my face. "It makes me happy to hear that, because I already miss you."

We kiss good night at my door. Before he turns to leave, he palms my face. "Good night, luv. I'll call you sometime tomorrow when I have a break. Will you be writing all day? I don't want to disturb you."

"Yes, I will be working, but it's fine. Call when you can. Good night, Bash."

I watch him drive off, realizing my hand is covering my mouth because of my feelings for him. I shake my head in disbelief. I change and get ready for bed, the whole time grinning like a teenager. Wondering about Bash, I think about our date that lasted the whole weekend. What will tomorrow bring? Tomorrow…writing. I grab my robe, head to my office, turn on my computer, and take the bottle of absinthe out of its hiding place. "I'm ready if you are, Prudence," I say to the dimly lit space around me. I open the bottle and take one sip, swallowing the liquid down.

CHAPTER NINE

The absinthe is very smooth this time, even more than before. There is no heat, no burn. Just the liquid's slightly medicinal but not unpleasant flavor, as if its once fiery nature had been cooled, somehow. *Or, am I just getting used to it?* I wonder.

On the other hand, it could be getting used to me. As it easily glides down my throat, I try to pay close attention to the mysterious effect it has on me. I feel as though I am being pulled somewhere. My head feels dizzy, and my limbs feel heavy; I just want to sleep…

***

Bernard packed up my daughters and took them to what I hope is a refuge from those who terrorize us. My Andrea, my little one, still so young and needing her mother; Suzette and Juliette, beautiful young ladies already. I wanted to teach each of them so much. To discover which of my girls would have their own particular healing abilities.

I determined to wait, to pray that I would get the chance to be with them again. But I never did. In the few days after Bernard and the girls departed for England, Lisette and I were occupied with the packing up of some personal belongings in the house. Lisette assured me our elixir was safe. She had also prepared an extra special one and placed it in a vile for me to ingest should I find that I must take fate into my own hands.

In the parish, my neighbors and those who I thought to be friends were turning on me. Even some of those who I had helped or had cured of their ailments, those who had thanked me when I had taken away their pain, would no longer even glance in my direction.

Some believed the witchcraft rumors to be true, and that Bernard and the girls had left me because of it. Others, who knew better, were just too petrified to associate with me for fear they would have brought pain and suffering upon themselves and their families.

I finally sent Lisette away, too, knowing that she would fare better within the security of her family. She fought against the idea at first, not wanting to leave me, but in the end she understood this was best. I sent with her certain amulets, powders, and lotions to aid her in the healing arts.

I told her to keep practicing her craft, to know the herbs and flowers of Mother Earth, to be guided to help heal the sick and clear away any dark energy she might encounter. I gave her a notebook of prayers, as well, entreating her to always meditate and to pray that even the most evil in this world might be healed and be brought to the ways of light by the benevolence I know is there. Now I was alone. All alone. I was so very afraid, and I missed my family.

I wondered where they were, how far they had gotten. I prayed I would see them again. My tears flowed on like a raging storm so that it was hard to catch my breath. I began to lose track of time, of the date. I only knew the air was becoming cooler and the days were getting shorter…

I am startled awake by the buzz of my cell phone. Startled, but not rattled. There are tears in my eyes. "I'm crying?" I ask myself softly. I quickly glance at the phone and find that it's nine a.m. Bash has sent a text.

Good morning, luv. Have a good day. Call you soon.

Bash.

I smile and swipe at my forehead. I move the mouse to bring my screen to life. "And there it is!" I shout. "Thank you, Prudence," I call out to an empty room (or is it?).

I read the latest entry. By the end of it, I am crying, again, and now realize this was the reason I had tears in my eyes when I awoke. "Oh God, Prudence! What happened?"

***

Doing extensive research and spending most of Monday back at the hall of records, I discover some history on Lisette's family, the Auberjeans. Their genealogy only goes back so far, but what I find is remarkable.

Racially and culturally mixed, Haitian and French, their status was a little higher here in Louisiana than it may have been elsewhere in America in the early nineteenth century. Instead of having to endure harsh slavery, they were paid for their work as butlers and maids in the wealthier family homes of the area's elite. They often earned respect and trust for their knowledge of healing the sick or helping the dying to cross over.

Some of the Auberjean women who came after Lisette practiced voodoo and were queens of their religion. Two men from Lisette's family line were what some considered to be witch doctors, but there is nothing more about them. I read all the way through and up to her grandmother being a respected voodoo queen. And, from what I already know, Lisette had the healer's gift.

Lisette was born in 1785 to a French farmer and his mistress, Marquette D'Arcy, a half-Haitian, half-French saint or princess whose mother was simply known as Delphine.

As I keep reading, I find out Lisette's grandmother's half-sister was the famous voodoo queen Marie Laveau, a voodoo celebrity around New Orleans. I continue to gather information and take notes. Then, to my surprise, I find out Lisette's descendants are still in the area and own an herbal shop in the French Quarter of New Orleans.

Excited by this information, I pack up my notebooks, put the record books away, and bolt out to my car. On the drive home I make a call to Bash.

"Hello, luv," he answers on the first ring.

"Hey," I say, "what do you have planned for tonight?"

"I have a bloody dinner meeting. I was going to call you soon and let you know. I told you, Mondays are crazy. Why? Did you have something in mind?"

"As a matter of fact, I do!" I tell him, my voice giddy with excitement. "I spent the day at the hall of records doing research for the book. I found out there is an herbal shop in New Orleans I want to visit. They may have answers to some of my questions."

"Sounds like you're a regular Sherlock Holmes! But, could we do this tomorrow instead? I pulled this meeting together tonight so I could spend tomorrow with you, and possibly the evening as well, before I leave for the airport on Wednesday."

I smile and shake my head. "Since you rearranged your day for me, I don't see why it can't wait. I would love to spend the day with you tomorrow in New Orleans."

"Great, luv. I can't wait. Should be fun to investigate this with you. Then I'll buy you a nice dinner in some quaint bistro and whisk you home straight away. I want to feel you all over me again. You're all I've thought about today."

"Sounds yummy, Bash—dinner too!" I joke. "What time can you pick me up?"

"Around ten?"

"Great! That works for me."

"All right, luv. I'll see you then. And...uh...Sharie," he adds, his voice sounding low and serious, "just be aware when I see you tomorrow we might get a late start. I may not be able to contain myself till evening."

I swallow hard and my heart thumps even harder, his words heating me all the way down to my core. I clear my throat and pull it together before I crash. "I'll be waiting, Mr. Devonshire. I'm already warmed up just thinking about it."

Just before he disconnected our call, I could have sworn I heard a low groan on his end of the line.

***

In the morning, I gather my notes and trinkets and put them in a folder with a clasp and pack some of the voodoo items in a satchel so they will be secure. I GPS the address, but I have a feeling Bash will know his way around New Orleans. I, on the other hand, have only been to New Orleans a few times, so I am a bit unsure of the area. Halfway through my morning latte, the doorbell rings. I check the time; nine-forty. He's early! I exclaim in my mind, and my belly does flip-flops in response.

I open the door, and Bash is standing there with some fresh cut flowers and a box of Dunkin' Donuts. "Morning, luv. For you." He hands me the flowers.

"Good morning," I answer, admiring the colorful array of blooms. I point to the box. "I hope there are some chocolate-cream filled doughnuts in there."

"Of course there are!" he says. He strolls past me to the kitchen table, where he opens the box. "There—see for yourself!" He motions with his hand. I reach in and snatch one, taking a big bite. Some of the chocolate cream ends up on the tip of my nose and Bash lifts my chin as I giggle. He licks it off, then wipes my mouth with his thumb, sucking at the creamy chocolate. "Adorable," he says as his deep sapphire gaze takes me in. My breath hitches, and I kiss him hard on the lips.

Bash lifts me in his arms and my legs wrap around his waist. *Jesus, what is it with this guy that gets me so turned on...?*

He sits down on one of my kitchen chairs with me still straddling him. I can feel he is just as turned on as I am. He puts his hands on my face, breaking our kiss. "You want me now, luv?" he whispers. "Or later? Tell me, Sharie." We are both breathing heavy. I reach up to pull my shirt over my head. As I do, he snaps open my bra and kisses my breasts. My fingers tangle in his curly hair. My heartbeat quickens and throbs down between my legs. "Tell me what you want!" he says with more force in his voice.

I reach for the button on his jeans, unzip them, and spring him free. "I want you, now," I moan. I stand to shrug off my pants while he fumbles frantically with a condom. He is about to stand up when I hold him there with a push of my finger and get back on top of him. I slide myself down slow, taking all of him in.

Our lips connect, and he groans into my mouth as our tongues twirl, still tasting of chocolate. I move my hips rhythmically, finding my pace. Bash has his hands around my waist, his fingers gently digging into my skin. I control every move. Bash watches me grinding on him with hooded eyes. "I'm close," I moan, and I feel his grip on me tighten.

"Me too, luv. God, I'm going to explode," he says tightly, struggling to get the words out.

The orgasm takes me hard. I tremble with pleasure. Bash groans through his teeth, still holding me tight. We stay still for a moment till the rush subsides. He leans me back to search my face, some of his curls fall into his eyes, and the smirk on his lips makes me self-conscious, and he can see it.

"No need to be shy, now, luv. You just seduced me in your kitchen."

I laugh but still feel timid. I can't believe how bold I am with him. I get up, grabbing my clothes from the floor.

"You asked for it," I say playfully.

"I did indeed, and you, my luv, are a brilliant lover."

"Brilliant lover." I cock my head to the side. "That's a first. Never been called that before, but I've never been with someone who brings out this wild side of me."

Bash stands to button his shirt. He grabs my hand and pulls me into him, his expression serious. "I know what you mean," he says softly then gives me a gentle kiss that touches my heart.

***

The drive into New Orleans doesn't take as long as we had anticipated. By the time we had left, the morning traffic had settled and we'd made it in twenty-five minutes as opposed to the forty-five we had calculated. Bash finds a place to park, and pays to keep our spot for the day. We check the address of the herbal shop and head toward the French Quarter.

Holding hands and strolling at a nice pace, we pass artists, musicians, and street performers doing their thing and entertaining pedestrians. From Bourbon Street to Royal

Street, the blocks are alive and electric with an aura that draws us in. We walk beneath balcony after balcony, waterfalls of colorful bouquets cascading above us.

The French Quarter's well-preserved architecture gives the area its beautiful charm, and I can see why it is a favorite with photographers. Above the sounds of some Dixieland jazz I say to Bash, "Says it's on Royal Street. We should be close." Bash takes the paper from my hand.

"May I?" he asks. "Eternal Herbs Botanical Healing Shop. Should be just around this corner." He points.

Soon, we are in front of the store. The windows display a crowded array of candles and books, pottery and stoneware. The door is mint green with an oval window. I turn the old-fashioned metal knob and we step inside. The scent of sage is clearly evident and hangs in the motionless air.

Lit candles, their flames bright and still, sit on shelves and tables. Open books are presented on podiums and pedestals. Shelf after shelf of bottles of liquids and powders are exhibited on one side; dried herbs tied in neat little bundles are stacked and displayed on the other. I glance at Bash. He is taking it all in, just as I am, when finally our eyes meet.

"Get a load of this stuff," he comments. "My God, I feel as though I've stepped back in time."

"Yeah, it's pretty cool, huh?" I say, a little mesmerized. I walk over to what I assume is a front desk. "Hello?" I bellow out. "Is anyone here?"

From somewhere in a back corner a voice says, "Hello, miss. I am here. What can I do for you, today?" My eyes take in a very thin but beautiful young woman, her skin the color of mocha cream, her eyes a light amber-hazel. Her hair is light brown with hints of blonde that seem so shiny they glitter in her spiral curls.

"Hello." I stick out my hand. "I'm Sharie Donovan, and this is Sebastian Devonshire. I'm writing a book, and I have been doing a lot of research for it, and what I found led me here. Are you, or do you know anyone who is, a descendant of Lisette Auberjean?"

The young woman's eyes pop wider and she smiles slightly. "Yes, she was my great-great-great-grandmother on my mother's side. My name is Brandy. What is it you are writing about, Ms. Donovan?"

"Well, I, uh…bought the old Ravensdale Manor, and some things were found when I renovated. I have a few of the things here with me and was hoping you could tell me about them. I also have a notebook containing what I assume to be Lisette's handwriting." Brandy reaches out to put her hand on my arm.

"I know it well. I know the stories that got passed around through the generations. Let me see what I can do. Come with me in the back." She looks over at Bash. "You'll have to stay here, though. Only one person allowed at a time."

"Oh, uh, that's fine." He hesitates. "I'll just step outside and make some phone calls about our dinner reservations." His eyes search my face, and he takes my hand. "You going to be all right in there?"

"Yes, I will be fine," I answer, looking at Brandy's pearly white smile.

"Right. I'll be just outside if you need me." Bash's eyebrow spikes in concern.

I almost burst into laughter. I can tell Bash is not comfortable here and not too pleased about letting me go off alone with Brandy. But, I feel fine about it. She seems sweet…secretive, but sweet.

CHAPTER TEN

As Bash leaves, I turn and follow Brandy around the counter and through the doorway's beaded curtain. I think, cliché, but keep my mind open. We walk down a dark hall to where it opens up to a bedroom-sized space. This area is decorated more ordinarily than the rest of the store. Two nice chairs with cushions and striped pillows sit in front of a coffee table. A matching love seat with a quilted pastel-colored blanket tossed on top sits across from them. A mid-sized picture window with shutters overlooks some sort of courtyard and lets in the early afternoon sun. White, wooden shelves of books line the pale-pink walls, along with framed posters of Jazz musicians and abstract art. More incense wafts through, this time with citrus added to the sage.

"Have a seat, please, Ms. Donovan. Not what you expected back here, is it?"

Slightly embarrassed, I give her a tight smile. "Not at all. I really like this room; it's cozy. And, please call me Sharie." I take the chair next to her.

"Thank you. I am here most of the day and night, so I need to have a place that is not so much for the tourists but normal, somewhere I can escape."

"Yeah, I get it," I tell her. Instantly, I feel even more at ease.

"I can make you tea or something, if you would like?"

"No thanks. I'm good."

"So, tell me, what have you found in Ravensdale Manor that brought you to me?" Her eyes twinkle as she smiles.

"Well...here." I open my satchel and pull out the pendant, the notebook, and some of the little brown bottles of powders. "These are just a few of the things. The notebook has prayers and other entries that I'm not familiar with, but I searched all I could about Prudence Ravensdale and Lisette at the hall of records. Like I said, your shop came up when I searched for more on the Auberjeans. Any help you can give me would be great!"

Brandy places all the Ravensdale paraphernalia on her coffee table then opens the powders and takes a sniff of each one. "Lemon balm," she surmises. Then, the next: "Hyssop!" She seems surprised. Finally, she flips through the notebook. "Hmm...here," she taps the paper with a French-manicured finger. "See this? It's a symbol for star anise. Tell me, Sharie, did you happen to find any bottles of a green elixir with this stuff or hidden anywhere else in the house?"

My stomach drops into my knees. "Umm...elixir? I...I..."

I'm fumbling, and she knows it.

"Sharie, it's okay. We are alone. One of the reasons I told your boyfriend that only you should come was because I sense you have a secret. And, if you do, I suggest you tell me. I am probably the only one who will understand and believe you."

"Yes, the elixir is there. How did you know?"

"The herbs in these bottles, the notes, plus the stories that have surrounded my family for generations. The elixir is absinthe."

I nod, "Yes, I have the bottle hidden in my desk drawer. I have actually sipped some of it." Her eyes go wide, and I feel like I've been busted for doing a bad drug.

"You drank it?" She put her hands to her face. "Tell me, have you gone on a trip? In your head, I mean."

I just stare at her, not even blinking.

"Oh sweet Jesus! You have!" "Oh my God, you must be thinking you've gone crazy."

As if I had been holding a breath, I exhale and feel a weight lift off of me. "At first, yeah, I did. But now, it's like she waits for me. She needs my help."

"At first?" She questions. "Oh shit, you drank more than once? And she waits? Who waits? Sharie—sit back, girl. You'd better tell me everything."

While I relate my whole story to Brandy, she nods here and there, smiles, and then sheds a tear. She stands and walks over to one of her bookshelves and pulls out a big, old, leather book. It looks heavy, and the pages are yellowish brown. She opens it up and brings it to the coffee table.

"This," she waves her hand over the book, "is my family-tree book. There are potions for healing, potions for fertility, recipes for foods and drink, and stories that have been passed down to me. I do not have a daughter, though there is still time. I have a son. He is twelve years old, but he hasn't shown any interest yet in what I do. Don't know if he will, but my grandmother and mother passed the gift down to me. My mom is still alive. She is gonna flip when she hears this! No worries, though—your secret is safe with us. Let me show you what I know."

Brandy flips through a few pages, reads silently, and then gives me a synopsis.

"Lisette, also a healer, met Prudence Ravensdale when she was still quite a young girl, herself. Back in those days, if you could find a family to work for that housed you, fed you, and you got paid"—she pauses—"whew! And, especially if you were a woman, that was like winning the lottery. Anyway, the story goes that when Lisette met Prudence they really clicked and became best friends. They shared the healer's gift, though some back then might have mistaken it for witchcraft. Here, they call it voodoo. The two of them knew how to make that absinthe the real way. It would help heal people when in pain and help ease the cough of bronchitis and consumption. They used a secret ingredient, but to this day no one knows what it was or if they were just that enchanted to be able to cast a spell on their elixir. It caused some folks to hallucinate.

Now, in your notebook, there are notes about being true of heart. Sharie, if Prudence is coming through to you, there is a reason. She is not at rest. Your heart must be pure for her to trust you. Let her tell you her story. She chose you for another reason, too, I'm sure. She knows you're a writer, and she needs her story told."

Brandy flips back a few more pages, reading to herself and following with her finger. I feel relieved and in a state of unbelievable wonderment, both at the same time. I'm also thinking about Bash. I would love to tell him about all this, but I seriously don't know how he will take it, and I'm pretty sure he feels this is all foolishness.

"Now, according to what I know, Prudence was murdered," Brandy proceeds, snapping my attention back to her.

"I thought she must have been," I say quickly. "All it said in the records was that her cause of death was unknown. But, after her last writing, I knew she had been in danger."

"Well, after Prudence died," Brandy continued, "Lisette returned to her family. She married and had children of her own, two girls. It is because of her we have this store. My great-great-grandmother Beatrice opened it here in 1890. The family has kept up with it, and we have made a decent living. Most who shop here are tourists, but there are also the gifted, who I keep a well-stocked inventory for."

"Brandy," I ask, "What about the men who wanted the secret ingredient? They killed Prudence for it, right? But, do we know how? And why didn't they pursue Lisette? She was lucky she got away."

"No, nothing further is written here about it, so I'm guessing they didn't know or they couldn't talk about it. All it says, here, is that they murdered her. Back then, if you were accused of witchery, they put down 'cause of death unknown' in town records to hide facts on purpose. Now, as

90

of great-great-great-grams Lisette, all I can tell you is back then the Auberjean family was big and powerful, and she sought the help of her grandmother, Delphine, a high priestess in her own right. They shuffled her around until she got married. By then, the danger was long past and she migrated back here with her family and lived a very long time, up to one hundred. Before she died, Lisette was able to work and share her craft with her great-aunt, her grandmother's half-sister, Marie Laveau."

I gape at Brandy with raised eyebrows. "Yes, I read that. She's a famous voodoo queen!"

Brandy laughs. "Yes, the one and only!"

"So, nowhere in that family-tree book of yours is the special ingredient in the absinthe that makes some of us crazy?"

"Unfortunately, no," Brandy giggles. "We have a saying: there are some things that must die with their maker. Sharie, you're not crazy; you're channeling a spirit. Whatever is in that recipe reacts with people differently. It must calm you enough to open your heart to let Prudence in. Usually, small children and animals can see spirits because their hearts are innocent. Some may hear them, but only if they are born with the gift.

"My niece! And her dog! They can see her!" I blurt out. "My niece Jaqueline is five—she can see her. She says Prudence stands by me when I work and that she is very nice but seems sad. And, that she points to a necklace she's wearing."

"Your niece told you this? Is this the necklace, here? The one with this pendant?"

"I don't know. I haven't had a chance to ask her. I just found out the other day that Jaqueline could see her. It was all I could do not to have a meltdown in front of her. I asked her to tell me exactly what she saw. I acted very calm so I wouldn't frighten her, but she says she's not afraid of her, anyway. It's our secret, for now, because I truly don't know how my sister and/or my boyfriend out there are going to handle this. I want to tell them when I have more information, though I don't see now how that makes it any better."

Brandy, sighing heavily, sits back in her seat. "They are going to find out eventually, and it may not be pretty. But, you have been chosen and that, Sharie, is a very high honor. Be careful."

She picks up the pendant and studies it for a minute or two then flips through more pages in her book. Brandy smiles and turns the book towards me. "Look." She points to a drawing of a cross with roses, just like the pendant I've found. "This," she says "is a protection amulet. Have you put this on at all?"

"Yes, the first night I sipped the absinthe. I thought it was pretty and figured it wasn't harmful—it's a cross! So, I guess I thought the same thing: protection."

"You are more pure of heart than you know, Sharie. This was Lisette's. Keep it with you always. It will protect you, keep you safe. I'm also going to give you some sage to burn. Light it and let the smoke go through the manor. When you sip the absinthe again and are open to channeling, this will keep any bad spirits from coming in. I think you have been pretty safe, but it doesn't hurt."

"Thank you so much for your time and your help, Brandy. Please, how can I pay you?"

Brandy looks up at me from her seat, her smile genuine. "I don't want your money. Learning all this is as fascinating for me as it is for you. Find out the whole story; write your book; give them justice and peace. God bless your journey, Sharie. You know where to find me if you need me."

I gather my things and tuck them all back into the satchel. We hug and exchange phone numbers. I feel better, maybe relieved that someone understands and believes what has been happening to me.

On the way out the door, I find Bash standing on the sidewalk watching an artist paint a picture. He spots me and comes to my side.

"How did it go?" He reaches for my hand and kisses my knuckles. "Was she able to give you some more information?"

"As a matter of fact, yes. It was very enlightening. Why don't I tell you about it over dinner, later? I'm still letting it sink in. Brandy is sweet, nothing to fear."

"Sounds great, luv. I thought we'd do a little more sightseeing, for now. Then, I have reserved a lovely table for us at a nice little bistro on the other side of Bourbon Street at about six."

"Works for me, Bash." I loop my arm with his and we go on our way. I decide I will tell Bash over dinner and some wine just some key parts of what Brandy and I had discussed today. No need to tell him the whole truth, yet, and now is not the time or place, anyway. I wouldn't even know how to begin that conversation. I realize I am falling for this wonderful man. I can't hide this from him too much longer, and truly I don't want to.

***

"This bistro is perfect, Bash. Dinner is fantastic! But, don't ever tell my sister I said that." We laugh.

"All your secrets are safe with me, luv. I hope you know that." Bash gets very serious for a moment as his facial expression seems pensive.

I place my hand over his. "I do, Bash. I think I really do."

He smiles wider and seems more at ease. I feel much more tranquil, myself. I really feel I can trust him with my secret. I decide I won't tell him until he returns from England. By then, I will have more of the story put together and hopefully an ending. I need more time with Prudence and more time to figure out how to explain everything to him. Confident with this decision, I relax a bit and smile at my thoughts. Bash takes notice and looks curious.

"What has got your pretty little mouth wearing such a grin, Ms. Donovan?"

I chuckle and toss back my hair. "I am just having a really good day, that's all. Things have come together. I got some answers, and then…there's you."

"Me? What about me, luv?"

"You crashed into my world like an earthquake. And, I'm scared…or was scared. I like my loneliness. The travel

94

thing you do I think will be good for us." Bash put up his hand to stop me.

"Sharie, you are a wonderful woman. In the short time we have been together, I've sensed you have a wall of ice up around you, but I'd like to believe I am melting it. I happen to be in awe of you and your family life. You're close with your sister. Your niece and nephew adore you. Your creativity, the way you've decorated the manor. All of it, Sharie. Even how passionate you are when we make love. I am drawn to you, and I don't want it to stop. You're what I have needed my whole life."

"How is that possible, Bash? You have everything." He put his napkin on the table and slowly shook his head.

"No, Sharie. I don't relish my loneliness as you do. Certainly, I have some family, but we were never close. I grew up with nannies and maids. I crave the very essence of where your family values are. Your parents may be gone, but they loved you. You are warm and full of fire. And that's where I want to be. Are you still afraid?"

"No, Bash, I was never afraid to have a relationship. I was afraid you thought I was someone I'm not."

Bash smiles. "Okay, luv, I have one more question for you." His face is serious, his voice stern and bold. "Do you want to stop and play pool for a bit on the way home, or do I need to get you home as fast as I can?"

I take a deep breath and look him right in those electric-blue eyes of his. "What do you think?" I ask on a shaky breath.

Bash shoots straight up from his chair, taking my arm. Escorting me out of the bistro, he whispers in my ear,

"Speed Racer it is, then." He helps me into the car and we drive off onto the dark highway. Every chance I get, I lean over to kiss and nibble at his neck, his ear. At one point, it seems he's thinking of pulling over right then and there but changes his mind and steps on the gas, instead.

Finally home, we race each other into the house and up to my bedroom. We fall, a tangled mess, onto the bed. Clothes flying. Hands searching. Mouths and tongues exploring each other's bodies. Bash secures me, snug in his arms. His kisses are even stronger, more demanding than they have been before. He breaks the kiss and we catch our breath. I want him. I crave him. He stares into my face. "Sharie," he says softly, "I was falling in love with you." His eyes never move from my face.

"Was?" I whisper. He kisses me softly.

"Yes," he answers. "Now I am in love with you. Please, don't be fearful."

I smile. With his face so honest and yet so serious, I can barely catch a breath to answer him. All I can flutter out is, "Me, too."

Bash sighs in relief; his kiss is hungry and full of longing. He fills me so smoothly, and our bodies become connected as one. His movements are hard and fierce with desire. I have never made love like this, so intense, in my life. His hips rock me till I feel the rush of heat roll through me like a wave as I hold on to him so tightly. When the orgasm hits, the charge is so hard, the cry that comes out of my mouth is so loud I don't recognize my own voice. Bash moans just as loud and we collapse in a heap, breathing heavy, soaked with sweat.

"I love you, Sharie. I know it's soon and fast, but this seems different. It's truly how I feel."

I curl up in his arms and kiss him tenderly. "For the first time, Bash, I feel a difference, too. More than I have ever felt before. I have fallen in love with you, too."

CHAPTER ELEVEN

Bash stirs from a deep and heavy slumber. Eyeing his surroundings, he quickly remembers he is in Sharie's bedroom. A big smile spreads across his face and a warm heat enters his chest. He reaches over to touch her, but the bed is empty.

"Sharie?" he calls out in a hushed tone. The room is too dark. Leaning over to find the lamp, he clicks on the light and his eyes adjust. "Sharie?" he calls a little louder. He gets up and shuffles his bare feet to the bathroom, "Sharie?" he repeats as he flicks on the lights. "Where could she be?"

Finding his boxer briefs and sliding them on, he makes his way out of the bathroom and down the hall. "Sharie, where are you?" Padding his way through the house, he sees light coming from Sharie's office. He hears her mumbling but can't make out what she is saying. "Sharie, are you writing? It's three-thirty in the morning. Come back to bed."

Moving closer toward her, he hears the keys on the computer tapping away. "Sharie—hey, luv—what are you working on?" He approaches her, puts his hand on her shoulder to turn her. "Sharie? SHARIE!"

***

I wake sitting at my computer once again. It's just at the break of daylight, earlier than usual. Then, I remember Bash had spent the night. After he had fallen asleep, I'd decided I could not wait until he left for England. I had to learn more of the story. So, I had tiptoed downstairs and taken a sip of the absinthe…

Thinking I'd better get back upstairs before Bash wakes up, I turn in my desk chair to stand—but Bash is sitting right there, fully clothed, glaring at me, and very pale in the chair next to mine.

Startled, I blurt out, "Bash! How long have you been sitting there?"

"Bloody long enough." His voice seems stern, and yet frightened.

I swallow hard. "Are you all right?"

"No, Sharie, I'm not. Last night, I came looking for you. I found you here, right at your desk, typing away."

The look on his face is complete horror. "Bash, I can explain."

"Really? Because, what I saw last night I cannot justify. I ruled out sleepwalking after I touched you, because I got knocked on my ass from a shock so strong from your body it rendered me nearly unconscious for fifteen minutes. Your

99

eyes were not normal; they appeared as though there was a white film over them, and as you typed you were looking off into the distance rather than at your screen. You could not hear me talking to you. You were in some kind of trance and mumbling—in French."

I am frozen to my chair, and my body feels like a thousand pins and needles are racing through my veins. Bash looks so confused, struggling to compose his demeanor, but his voice cracks with what must be tones of anger, fear, and disbelief. His eyes are slightly bloodshot, and he can't really look me in the eyes.

"Sharie," he murmurs, barely audible. "I thought…maybe lunacy, some kind of insanity, a brain tumor. But I fear it is beyond normality. So, I stayed and watched you till you passed out. But I dread, now, to hear what you could possibly say to explain what I witnessed."

I take a deep breath and stand. I take a few steps in his direction, and he puts up his hand. "Bash, don't be afraid! I'm all right!" I sit back down and pull my chair slightly closer so I can face him. "It's all going to be fine. Actually it's a pretty amazing story."

I fumble along, stuttering my words. He is frightened of me and won't let me near him. "The voodoo things I found? I…I…am channeling Prudence's spirit. She trusts me, she needs my help. She…she was murdered, and…"

"SHARIE!" he yells, his tone striking me like a slap. "That's insane! You mean you're possessed? I am finding this way too bizarre to handle."

"Bash, it's okay! I swear I am the same person you know. Please let me help you understand!"

Bash stands and puts up his hands. "I can't do this, Sharie. I don't understand what kind of shit is going on here, but I just can't..." He shakes his head. "Jesus, Sharie, are you not afraid of what is happening to you? That you just believe it all to be fine and true?"

"Of course I'm scared, or was...I'm catholic; I believe in anything that scares me," I say, half-joking, hoping to smooth things over.

"You're joking?" He puts a hand through his messy hair. "You think this a bloody joke? I'm not laughing, Sharie. I sat here awake all night, watching you. I couldn't do anything to help you! Sitting here, scared shitless, waiting for you to come out of wherever you were and hoping to God your head wouldn't spin and spit green goo!"

I put my hand over my mouth but can't contain a giggle. Bash's eyes grow wide; this is absolutely not funny to him at all. I feel bad and try to put myself in his shoes, but I know I would be more open-minded. I would give him a chance to explain. He won't let me get a word across. I'm getting pissed!

"Bash, please. You're shutting me out!" I yell. "There is no danger. I am fine. Please sit down. I'll make us coffee. I'll explain everything. Actually, I'm relieved now that you know. I was going to tell you but was afraid you wouldn't understand. But, last night, you told me my secrets are safe with you. You told me you loved me, so now I'm letting you in. Maybe you can help."

Bash hangs his head as if in defeat. "Help? You need divine help. You're being possessed. And, just when were you going to tell me? Over dinner one night? Pass the butter...and, oh, by the way, I forgot to tell you I share my

101

body with a bloody demon! You're like Jekyll and Hyde! I don't know how to help you, Sharie!"

"She's not a demon. Please, Bash, let me explain!" My voice gets louder.

"You know the demon is a she? Oh, that's right. You think it's Prudence Ravensdale, who has been dead for two hundred years! For fuck sake, do you realize how crazy this sounds?"

Now I am totally enraged. He's not listening.

"I know it's her. Why won't you give me the chance to tell you what is going on?"

"Sharie, I don't—or can't—even fathom this rubbish, and, quite frankly, I'm finding it hard to trust you, right now. I must leave. I don't know when I'll be back. Please don't call me; I need time to think."

I hold in a sob that's about to erupt, but tears pool in my eyes. "GET OUT!" I scream and point to the door. "I knew you were too good to be true. You told me you loved me, that my secrets were safe with you. Really? If you loved me, you wouldn't leave. But, you know what, Bash? GO! Get the fuck out! I don't need you. You can have all the time in the world. The hell with you! And, Bash, don't worry—I've already lost your number."

Bash stares at me for a moment, but I turn my head away in disgust. He stomps out of my house. When I hear the door slam, I let my tears fall.

***

I let myself have a good cry while soaking in a hot bubble-bath till I prune up and am all cried out.

I put on my coziest yoga pants and an oversized, soft shirt. I make a cup of tea and take it down to my office. I sit sipping, thinking, getting angry. I will give myself the rest of the day to lick my wounds and feel sorry for myself, but that's it. I am just getting more furious at the way Bash and I left things. I can't imagine how frightened he must be. However, he wouldn't even give me the chance to explain.

Going through the argument in my mind, over and over, I can put myself in his place, sure, but I would have listened to reason. And I wouldn't have walked out on someone I love. My secrets are safe with him, he told me. Hah!

My thoughts scrambling, I suddenly comprehend what he saw and heard. He said I was speaking in French. "I don't know French!" I say to myself, wondering what I said. My eyes went white? I get up and look in the mirror. I don't know what I expected to see, but of course, I appear normal. "He was shocked by some kind of energy and knocked unconscious!" I turn my attention to my computer and stumble over to it, move the mouse, and there are Prudence's words. I reach for my mug of tea, sit down, and read the entry.

I had sent for Lisette days ago to help arrange a strategy, knowing I must vanish from this place, secretly. That night was the date we had set, the 10th of November. I was waiting in the chilly air on the path in the woods beyond the house. Lisette was to bring me a change of clothes so I could disguise myself and easily slip out to the streets and head toward the harbor. By dawn, I was to board the same ship that had taken my husband and children to England. I so dearly longed to reunite with them.

I heard Lisette whispering my name through the brush. She reached me and was holding a basket of clothes she'd confiscated from the convent. I slipped on the robe of a nun's habit, its veils long enough to hang over my face. As Lisette helped me in the dark, we spoke no words. When I was ready, we hugged for the last time; I would never see my Lisette again.

She handed me the vile of the special elixir and I placed it in the pocket of the habit. We stood there for just a moment before Lisette urged me to go. She had seen Dubied's men in the pub, drunk and raising hell. I thanked her, gave her one last hug, and she was gone.

I took the path past the big oak and on to the street, carrying only a leather travel case in my hand containing a few of my personal items. Before long, I heard the gallop of a horse behind me. I didn't look, but the rider moved his horse in my way.

"Where you going, sister?" he asked in a raspy, inebriated tone. "You are a little distance from the convent. Are you lost?"

"I was visiting a sick parishioner," I answered him. "I am not in need of your assistance. Please move so that I may pass."

"Well, sister, that's one hell of a sweet French accent you have. Who did you say you were visiting?"

"I didn't say. Now, please get out of my way, sir, so I can continue on my errand." I kept my head low, partially hidden by the veils. I would not look the stranger in the eyes. I knew who he was. I know, now, they had been watching.

"You wouldn't have been visiting the witch, now, were you? I hate to think one of God's messengers was friendly with the filthy Ravensdale witch."

"My affairs are no concern of yours. Now, if you please, I will be on my way." My heart pounded hard. I was terrified.

"You're not going anywhere, WITCH!"

Before I realized what was happening, more men on horseback had surrounded me. They knew who I was. One grabbed me up, slung me across his horse's withers, and took me, screaming, back into the woods. In the darkness of the forest, he pushed me roughly off the horse and I dropped onto the dirt.

I struggled to run, but another man pushed a pistol to my head to stop me. Others, then, held me up against a giant oak tree and proceeded to hang a rope from its branch. The raspy-voiced man came so close to my face that I could smell the whiskey diffusing from his pores.

"Now, Monsieur Dubied has commissioned us to get something he wants. We have asked kindly, but you just don't want to cooperate. Gonna ask you again: give us the whole recipe for the absinthe." As he spoke he had placed a finger on my face and was tracing along my jaw and throat.

So petrified I could barley breathe, I told them I had given Dubied everything, that he already had the full recipe, that there was nothing more.

Cornelia…chene…collier…

collier…grand chene…

…Cornelia…

He put his finger around the necklace that held a locket given to me by my husband and daughters and tore it from my neck. He opened it and saw the tiny portrait of my family.

"They left you, witch. Your own family knows what you are. We're gonna do them a favor and get rid of you. This is no place for an evil witch."

Feeling such hatred for this man and his cronies, I spat in his face.

"You are a living evil," I said boldly, "and Dubied is the devil himself getting you to do his bidding." He tossed my locket into the bushes and punched me hard in the face. I felt the hot, *sticky blood slide from my nose as the pain between my eyes blurred my vision and I collapsed on the ground in a heap. I tried to focus around me as best I could.*

The men were knotting the rope and drinking more from their flasks. As if from a distance, I heard them talking. They were going to take turns, hold me down, and each would have his way with me. I reached in my pocket and pulled out the tiny, delicate vile Lisette had made for me. With the slight force of my thumb, I was able to break the seal.

Rolling over slowly to turn my back to them, I carefully put the vile to my lips and sucked the liquid down. I felt it tingle and then calm me. Very soon, I drifted past life's dark veil and woke on the other side. The men thought I had just been knocked out by the punch, but my essence had already moved on. They tried waking me, grabbing beneath my skirts, ripping the nun's habit from my breasts. Finally, they gave up.

They hung me from the rope, unaware of my demise, and watched as my body swung from the big oak until they had tired of the spectacle and left me there in the darkness.

I read this entry through stinging tears I try to wipe away. When I finish, I scroll back to the break in Prudence's story. The name *Cornelia* is written along with the words *grand chene* and *collier*. "What does this mean?" I ask aloud. "And who's Cornelia?" I sit there reading it over and over, trying to comprehend, taking mental notes: A path beyond the house, a big oak tree, *grand chene*. A necklace with a locket, *collier*. "French!" I jump up, slip on my sneakers, and run out my back door and into the woods. I find the path, amazed it is still there after all this time, and follow it until I come to the biggest oak tree I've ever seen.

I glance around at the whole scene in front of me. I hear light traffic in the distance, and I realize it's the end of my street going on to one of the main highways. That street must be the same one where Prudence's killers stalked her. The men on horseback, nearly two hundred years ago.

I gaze at the giant oak tree before me. A feeling of complete sadness seeps into my body. Overwhelmed with emotion, I kneel on the ground and just absorb it all. This is all so surreal but, at the same time, almost tangible.

I stay there for minutes, hours, not really aware of how long. I find myself at the manor and don't remember walking back home. My thoughts race between Sebastian and Prudence, to Brandy and Lisette, to Jaqueline.

I sit on a bench in my courtyard, so deep in thought I become exhausted. Finally, after standing and stretching my muscles, I enter the house. I check the time and realize hours have gone by. Soon, the sun will set.

I will not hear Bash whisper, "Good night, luv," to me on the phone this evening. As much as I hate to admit it, I love him; it's killing me. Also, I cannot bear to read any more of Prudence's story for a day or two. I need a break. I'm drained and getting fatigued.

I grab one of my favorite books: *Wifey*, by Judy Blume. I have loved her books since I was a teen. I get into bed with the smutty and funny novel, hoping it will help me to focus elsewhere, decompress, shut off my brain for a while.

As I crawl into bed, my cell phone bleeps. It's my sister. Charlotte will just have to wait until tomorrow. She's going to want to know how things are going. If I even begin to think about that conversation tonight, my head will explode for sure.

CHAPTER TWELVE

Cornelia Devonshire stares at her son from across the giant dining table as they eat breakfast. She can tell there is something not right with her son.

When Sebastian arrived home two days prior, he seemed preoccupied and agitated. He hadn't wanted to talk and seemed to mope about the place in a state of depression. Today, the silence during breakfast is excruciating for Cornelia. Usually, she and Sebastian have a multitude of topics to chat about—some business, some fun—but she has never seen him so far away before.

"Son, please talk to me. I can see there is a heavy weight on you. Tell me what is burdening you so."

Sebastian throws his napkin on the table and sits back in his chair, gripping the lion's-paw armrests at each side. His gaze narrows at his mother. He ponders for a moment. "I don't know where to begin," he blurts.

"Is it that girl? The one who bought the manor?" she asked, coaxing him to talk. "Are you in love, dear?"

"Yes," he answers softly. "I love her, but it's something beyond that." Sebastian swipes at his forehead then grabs a clump of his hair and stares, unseeing, at his plate of uneaten food.

"You have barely touched your food. Has there been an argument of some kind?"

Slowly, he raises his eyes to his mother. "I have seen something I cannot explain. Mother, you are going to think I'm insane. Sharie is somehow being possessed. I have seen this thing inside of her, controlling her. When I tried to touch her, I was physically jolted so hard it blew me off my feet!"

Cornelia stands very slowly and remains calm. She quickly remembers the house speaking to her on occasion and how it had frightened her so. "Sebastian, what did you see? What has happened?"

Exasperated, he shakes his head from side to side. "I wish I knew, Mother. I truly am trying to make sense out of the whole bloody thing. I witnessed Sharie sitting at her computer, typing away, but she wasn't there, you know? It wasn't her. She was in some kind of a trance. Something or someone had taken hold of her, making her type. She was even babbling on in French, but her voice was muffled. When she came out of it, she seemed to be fine, kept telling me she could explain, like she knew what's going on. She didn't even seem frightened! Can you imagine? We definitely had some words. I felt so helpless; I just needed to get out of there. I am at a complete and utter loss. I don't know what to think."

"Sebastian Charles Devonshire," Cornelia articulated sharply, "you saw this happening and you left that girl alone in that house? I knew we should have torn it down."

"Mother, what are you talking about? Is there something you're not telling me about that house?"

Cornelia's eyes wandered off. "It's all my fault." Her voice was low. "I should have made your father tear down that house, but he wouldn't hear of it. Then you," she pointed. "I should have pleaded with you to tear it down, but you talked me into selling it. Now, it is haunting someone not even of our family bloodline."

"Mother, what the bloody hell are you saying?"

"Ravensdale Manor. It is haunted. It used to speak to me, and to your grandmother, and to her mother before her. The men never hear it. When I first married your father, we would spend many a holiday there. I would tell him I heard someone whispering my name over and over in a French accent. He told me I was imagining it. One morning, before you were born, your grandmother asked me if I had heard the voice, yet. I played it off like I didn't know what she was talking about; she knew I was lying, of course. But, same as you, I couldn't believe it. Grandmother told me only some women hear the voice of Prudence Henriod Ravensdale, whether they are related directly through the bloodline or marry into it. Then she told me the story of our ancestor, Prudence.

As Cornelia continues, Sebastian sits almost in shock over his mother's confession.

"According to the story, Prudence was murdered for being a witch and even her husband abandoned her and left her for dead. So, her spirit has been unable to find peace."

110

Sebastian's eyes grow wide. "Oh my God! I left her there. I was so scared, stupid, and completely confused. I knew we had a family history, but a haunted one? I left the woman I love in that house! I need to get her out of there. You should have told me what you knew! For Christ's sake, how could you have kept this information from me?"

"Because, usually, men don't hear or see her. Your father and I fought too much about that house, so I just stopped going. I thought you wouldn't believe me either, and I didn't want to fight with you, too. But, you have seen the spirit of Prudence! Sebastian, what was Sharie typing while being inhabited by the spirit?"

"I don't know. I didn't stay. I feel like a real shit, now, because I walked out. I told her I needed time to wrap my head around this. I...I don't think she's afraid, though. I think I heard her say something about helping her—Prudence. I can't really be sure about it."

"Call Sharie, son! Tell her to get out of the house and that you're coming to get her. We'll have that place demolished!"

"I'm not sure she's going to want to talk to me; I was really a wanker. I'm so stupid! I was not the man I should have been. She threw me out."

Cornelia gazes upon her son, and her face relaxes at the sight of him. "Seems to me you have met your match." She feels sorry for him and is determined to help make things right. "Does she love you, too?"

"Yes, I believe so. We had an intimate conversation just the night before, but after what transpired I'm not sure what her feelings are now."

"Nonsense!" she spurts. "Call her. Tell her you love her and you were wrong. Tell her you know more now and you understand, and that we're coming to get her!"

Sebastian grabs for his cell phone, but just before he taps in Sharie's name, he eyes his mother's serious face. "What do you mean we're coming?"

"I'm coming with you. I may be able to help."

***

A knock on my door interrupts my thoughts as I bang away on my computer keyboard. I hear the front door open. "Sharie! I'm coming in." I take a deep breath before answering.

"I'm down in my office, Charlotte!" I hear my sister and niece trample through my house and make their way down to greet me. I brace myself for what is about to happen.

"Hi, Auntie Shree!" Jaqueline runs towards me with her arms wide open and Friedo close behind. I swivel my chair and snuggle her up in my arms. I breathe her in. She smells like powder and strawberries and is a welcome surprise. I realize how much I've missed her this week. I glance behind her. My sister is another story, standing there, arms folded, eyebrow raised up to her hairline.

"I haven't seen or heard from you since Saturday! Eight days later, here you are, alive! Thank God. I call you, and all you have done is send me back shitty text messages saying '*busy not now*.' Spill it, sister: What's going on with you?"

112

I pause and shake my head. "Sebastian left, so I'm diving into work, nothing to worry about." I give her a tight-lipped smile.

"Bullshit!" Charlotte spits. She looks at her daughter, who's making tisking sounds..."Ooh, Mommy says two bad words."

"Yes, I said bad words. Go upstairs, Jaqueline, and watch T.V. Mommy and Auntie Sharie need to have a big-girl talk."

We both watch as Jaqueline and Friedo leave us. When my sister hears the T.V. go on, she plops down on one of the wingback chairs and motions me toward the chair next to her. "What's really going on with you? Did you and Bash have a falling out?"

"Yes, and that's that. End of story."

"Sharie, what happened?"

"Let's just say I don't think he is good at handling serious situations."

"Are you going to tell me what the hell happened, or am I going to have to beat it out of you? Stop being so vague!"

"OKAY! Fine. Here goes. I'm going to tell you the God's honest truth. Please don't think I'm crazy till you have heard the whole thing. First, I need you to read what I have been writing. It's all part of what I have been going through."

***

113

I sit quietly, waiting for my sister to finish reading what I've been working on. When she's done, she smiles and turns in her seat.

"Sharie, I love it so far. I can't wait to read the rest. Do you have an ending ready?"

"Not yet," I tell her. "You see, it has not been told to me, yet."

"You writers amaze me," Charlotte says. "The way you get so caught up in your characters and they 'talk' to you. You must have some kind of idea, though, where this going, don't you?"

I shake my head. "No, not really. Not this time."

"And, this is different now…why? Okay, Sharie, I'm all ears."

I stand and pace over to my desk and retrieve the bottle of absinthe out of my desk drawer. I place it in her hands. "This is the reason this time is different." She reads the label then shrugs at me, confused. "Charlotte, I'm about to tell you something so incredible you'll have a hard time believing it. Please keep an open mind."

I begin to share my experience, starting with the workmen finding the desk containing the voodoo items. I tell Charlotte how Prudence has been telling her story through me when I drink the absinthe, how I believe her unsettled spirit needs my help.

I talk about Brandy from the herbal shop and all the things she divulged to me, including her theories about why Prudence chose me for this. My sister listens to all of it and never says a word. Her eyes seem to never blink, and her mouth is slightly open.

I continue by telling her about Sebastian finding me a few nights ago, right here at my desk, while Prudence's spirit was speaking through me...and how scared he was. How, even though we had confessed our love for one another just the night before, he hadn't known how to handle this and had simply walked out. Finally, with a glance at my sister, I nervously call to my niece and ask her to come downstairs.

"What do you need with Jaqueline?" Charlotte questions.

"You'll see. Please stay calm, and remember there's nothing to fear."

My niece comes down the stairs with Friedo wagging his fluffy tail behind him. "Jaqueline, remember the little secret we have?" She nods. "We're going to tell your mom about it, now."

"K, Auntie Shree. The lady is happy that we are here. She's smiling."

"What is she talking about?" my sister asks. She is calm, so far, and seems intrigued.

"Charlotte, your daughter can see Prudence's spirit. And I believe Friedo can, too." We all take notice as the dog sits there wagging his tail and whining at the wall.

My sister leans over in her chair and gets closer to her daughter. "Jaqueline, baby, tell mommy who you see. It's okay. I am not mad, and you are not in trouble."

"The lady over there." She points with her tiny hand. "Friedo sees her. She is happy today."

I move closer to Jaqueline, too. "Can you hear her, sweetie?" I ask.

"No." She shakes her head. "She tries to talk, but it sounds like a buzz. She points to stuff and waves at me and Friedo."

"Is she pointing to anything now?" Charlotte asks.

Jaqueline looks over to the wall. "Her necklace, and then out the window."

"She's pointing out the window? Why?" I ask my niece. "Is there something outside?"

Jaqueline shrugs her shoulders. "I don't know, Aunt Shree. Today, she just points to her necklace and then the window."

"Wait a minute," Charlotte says, putting up her hands. "What does she do on other days? How long have you been seeing her?"

"I don't know. She's always here watching Aunt Shree type, and she's always looking out that window. Maybe she wants to go outside."

"Outside!" I shout. I go over to the door. "Can Prudence get outside, Jaqueline?"

She nods. "Yep, she just did."

We all go out onto the little patio. "Where is she now, Jaqueline?" I ask.

"Over there, near the woods. She's pointing to them."

I glance at my sister. "Oh dear God," she says. "It's the path to the tree you just told me about."

"Come on! I'll take you to it."

On our way toward the big oak, I turn to my sister. "So, you believe me, us, and everything?"

"Yes, but I am very pissed off you didn't tell me sooner, Sharie. How dare you not let me in on this! How cool is this? And, seriously, what did you think I was going to do? I'm your sister. I can't believe you and my own daughter kept this from me. To go on with this by yourself. I just hope I never see Bash again. He must be a very weak-minded person to have walked out the way he did."

"No—just scared, Charlotte, and helpless. I believe Bash is not used to being unable to control a situation. You should have seen his face. He truly was completely torn."

"You haven't heard from him since?"

I roll my eyes. "He tried to call me once and he sent a couple messages, but I blocked him. I love him, but I can't deal with him right now."

"Well, maybe you should see what he wants."

"From what his text said, he thinks I'm in danger and wants me to get out of the house. I tried to tell him I'm not in any danger, but he wouldn't listen."

"She's here!" my niece squeals. "She beat us here."

"What is she doing, Jaqueline?" I ask.

"She's pointing to the tree and then over there to that bush."

My sister looks around. "Is this where it happened?" she asks me quietly. I just nod. We don't want to frighten Jaqueline, but I have to admit the kid's a trooper.

"What is she doing now, baby?" my sister asks.

"She's gone," Jaqueline tells us. "She went over to that bush, and she's just gone."

"Did she vanish, you know, disappear?" I ask her.

"Yep, just like a real ghost," she says with a smile.

My sister picks up her daughter and carries her on her hip. "Your Mommy's brave, big girl, you know that?"

Jaqueline giggles. "She's not scary, Mommy."

I walk over to the bush, though it seems more like a plant, with big, green leaves and pretty, light-purple, tulip-shaped flowers holding big black berries. Some of the berries are still green but starting to ripen. I walk around the plant and notice nothing more than just the wooded area and grassy ground around it. "I wonder why she would just disappear?"

"Does it say anything in the notebook about it?" my sister asks.

"No, but there are some drawings of the tree. I'd like to call Brandy, get her out here to see what she thinks." Charlotte nods in agreement. "I'll call her first thing in the morning."

CHAPTER THIRTEEN

Sebastian keeps checking his cell. Cornelia keeps watching her son fidget in his seat. "She still hasn't answered you?"

"No, I told you the argument didn't end well. I don't even think she has listened to my messages." He tosses his phone onto the little tray table and looks out the window. "We should be landing by morning. Try to get some rest, Mum."

"I believe you should do the same, dear. Some sleep will do you good." She pondered a moment. "Sebastian, you know you have met someone you can't control. Sharie sounds feisty. That's probably what you love about her."

Glancing at his mother, he gives her a sympathetic smile. "I suppose that could be true." He sits back and tries to close his eyes. "I can't sleep. Not until I talk with Sharie. Not until I fix what I've done."

***

I watch my sister and Jaqueline pull out of my driveway. I am so pleased my sister now knows everything. Spending the day with her and my niece, talking over what's been happening, was a welcome relief. Her understanding and believing have calmed me. I don't feel like I have lost my mind, anymore. I walk back to my kitchen, where we had spent most of the afternoon talking about Bash and raiding the fridge. While we chatted over some chocolate-chip mint ice cream, Charlotte had prepared some chicken roulade for my dinner. It is now roasting away in the oven, and the smell is mouthwatering. I check the timer: just ten more minutes and I'll feast! I pour a glass of wine as thoughts of Bash swirl through my head. I grab my phone. The last text he sent said:

I Love you, I'm so sorry, forgive me.

I sigh, and tears prick my eyes. The sound of the oven timer pulls me from my daze, and I take out my dinner.

After cleaning up the kitchen, I think about going out to the restaurant for some drinks, to be around people and laugh a little. Usually, my brother-in-law can put a smile on my face, but the more I think about things, the more Prudence enters my mind. "Okay, Prudence," I say aloud, "guess it's you and me tonight."

Down to my office I go. I sit at my computer, open the drawer, and take out the bottle of absinthe. I pull the cork and come to a startling halt. The bottle is almost empty. How did I not notice? What little is left I hope will still allow me to be open enough to channel Prudence's spirit. I lift the bottle to my lips and suck down the last, small drop. This stuff usually has some punch with just one sip, but what I've just had is more like only a taste. I still feel a familiar warmth, though, as I swallow the tiny amount.

I sit and wait, but nothing happens. I almost want to cry. I really didn't think about running out of the elixir, I was so focused on helping Prudence and finishing the book. I open the file titled *Ravensdale Manor* and read to where I had left off, or rather where Prudence had left off. Suddenly, ever so slightly I start to see images. They are fuzzy and going in and out. I am partially in Prudence's world and partly in mine. I try to concentrate. My fingers automatically type:

Big oak. Find me. Locket. Home.

This is it. I'm not going into a trance this time. It's all so sketchy.

"Prudence," I call out into the empty room, "I don't understand. I am trying to find you. I'm out of the absinthe. It wasn't enough, and I barely comprehend what you're trying to show me."

In a moment, my half-transitional state is gone—all at once, as if a rubber band had been pulled back and let go, snapping me back. I feel as though I'm a rock in a slingshot, but with no target. Emptiness surrounds me. For the first time since I've lived in this house, I swear I feel its sadness.

I have gotten so close to it all, to Prudence's life and death. All I can do now is work. I find the little notebook and go through it page by page, searching for some hint, a clue. I read again the last entry that Prudence gave to me. I make some outlines and secondary notes until I can't see straight any more. Worn out and tired, I decide to call it quits and go up to bed.

***

Dark and foggy. My bare feet tiptoeing on dewy, wet grass. Still wearing my night shirt. What am I doing here? Oh, the big oak tree—I see it. I feel a presence. "Who is there?" I call out, feeling vulnerable and confused. I hear footsteps. "Someone there?" I call out again, and my voice cracks in fear. I don't like it here, now. I'm going home. As I turn, I hear a buzzing like radio static, but I perceive my name in the noise. I turn back.

I see a figure all in black floating towards me. I try to move, but I am immobile, frozen to the ground in fear. The figure is a woman, a nun. "Prudence?" I whisper. I can't see her face. She holds out a skeletal hand. A silver necklace with a heart-shaped pendant hangs from the bony, spine-like fingers. She points to the tree and then the plant with the dark berries. "What is it, Prudence?" I ask. I can barely talk or breathe. A louder hiss of static crackles in my ears.

I awake in bed.

"Oh thank God. I'm dreaming." I sit up and see a skeletal head wearing a nun's habit at the foot of my bed.

The sound of my own scream brings me back to reality. Sitting up, I scan around my empty room. The sun is just breaking through. I rub my face. My heart is pounding into my ears, and I need to catch my breath. "Holy shit!" I blurt. "What a nightmare...or was it?" I lean over to check the time: seven-thirty a.m. I get up to get a glass of water. I contemplate calling Brandy within an hour.

***

Sebastian's and Cornelia's flight lands at eight a.m. They drive to the condo and freshen up. One more time, Sebastian sends a call to Sharie and finally, to his surprise, she answers.

"Bash?"

"Hello, luv. Can we please talk?"

"We can, if you are ready to listen. I love you, Bash, but I can't be with someone who won't even give me a chance to explain something without running off. I know you were frightened—believe me, I get it—but you completely shut me out."

"Sharie, I'm so sorry. I was stupid, a complete wanker. Can you ever forgive me? I missed you so much. I can't stand being away from you. I'm here, back at the condo, and Mother is here with me. She explained things about the house I never knew. We think you need get out of there right away. It's not safe, and I'm coming to get you!"

"Wait, Bash! No, I don't need to leave. I'm fine. What has your mother told you?"

"She told me the house used to speak to her and my grandmother, as well as the women in the family before them. It frightened her so much that she never wanted to go to the house again. She told me a horrible story. I believe you're in danger if you remain in that house. Our ancestor, Prudence, was a witch, and…"

"NO, Bash, she was not a witch!" Sharie let out a big sigh. "You and your mother need to come here. I need you both to see what I have written. It explains so much. I promise you, there is no danger at all. You've got to believe me. No arguing this time. I will explain everything, including what you saw."

"We can be there in an hour. But, Sharie, if I don't like what I hear and I still think it's dangerous, I'm taking you away from there."

He hears an impatient groan. "Bash, I don't need you to save me, I need you to believe me."

He considers the thought. "All right, luv," he replies softly. "See you soon."

Bash hangs up the phone and knows his mother has been eavesdropping. "I know you're listening, Mother. We are going over there." Cornelia comes to the entrance of his room and leans against the door. Bash eyes her for a moment. "She's asked me to trust her."

"She's being manipulated by a demon, I'm afraid. We won't know what to believe. I just know that once I was away from there I felt better."

Feeling a bit frustrated between trying to respect his mother's wishes and trying to believe the woman he loves, Sebastian knows he at least needs to give Sharie her chance. "I do love her, and I'm going to let her explain. It's the least I can do after the way I left. If you don't want to come, I'll understand, but I will hear her out. Do I make myself clear?"

Cornelia gazes at her son. "Yes, son. Crystal clear. At least you're going to try; your father just thought I was mad. Can't say I'm not worried about the whole thing—and if I hear one little word in my head, I'm leaving."

***

124

I'm so glad I finally talked with Bash. The best thing I ever did was give ourselves that week to let things calm down, though. If I had spoken with him too soon, I still would have been too angry to work anything out. I can't even say I'm totally over Bash's reaction, yet, so I'll wait and see how today goes before I make any assumptions about our relationship.

I decide to call Charlotte and ask if she and her family would like to come over, too. I tell her about Bash's return and that he and his mother will be here soon.

"I think it will help if I have everyone here," I say.

"Bash's mom came, too? Holy hell, this is how you're going to meet his mother for the first time?"

I laugh, "Yes, I know…how weird. But, apparently, the house used to talk to her, too."

"Did you call Brandy?" my sister asks.

"Yeah, she's coming over tomorrow night after she closes the shop. I was hoping she would come today in the daylight. I had a nightmare last night about that big oak. It was all dark and foggy…I'm still getting the creeps."

"Don't get too spooked. I'm sure it was just a dream. You've got a lot going on, Sharie. Let me round up the troops, and we'll head over as soon as possible. I'll stop by the restaurant and bring some supplies to make everyone brunch."

"Oh, Charlotte, you don't have to. I have food here you can use."

I hear her snort. "Sharie. First of all, I was there yesterday; I was in your fridge. Trust me, you need my

125

help, and you have Bash's mother coming, so let's make a good impression, or try to, anyway."

"Thanks, sis. You're the best!"

I disconnect our call and look around the house, realizing I have been slacking in the cleaning department this week. Quickly, I start to pick up empty beer bottles and pillows that had fallen on the floor. I run the vacuum, then dust. Finally, I sprint upstairs for a fast shower.

Before I am completely presentable, the doorbell rings. I am so nervous! I open the door, and there is Bash, looking handsome in relaxed jeans and a black shirt. His hair is tousled from the wind, and he is clean shaven and smells of spice and leather. His eyes look tired and a bit red with faint dark circles under them. The petite woman next to him has soft, grey hair parted on the side and cut in a perfect bob. She's dressed in tan slacks, a lightweight, white, knit top with buttons, and a light-blue scarf held in place by a diamond brooch. She looks sophisticated and refined but also appears very nervous. Bash takes one look in my eyes and reaches for me.

"Sharie." He pulls me to him and hugs me, tight. "I'm so sorry, luv! Can you forgive me?"

"Bash, it's all right. It's over. Let's just move on."

He puts his hands on my face and brushes his lips over mine a few times until his kiss becomes deep and poignant. I can feel his sorrow and regret. I put my arms around him and kiss him back like it is crucial to my existence.

"Ahem…"

Bash steps aside with a smirk. "Sharie, luv, this is my mother, Cornelia Devonshire."

"Hello, it is so nice to meet you." I put out my hand to shake hers, and her name slaps my brain, sending a chill up my spine. The look on my face must be frightful.

"Sharie, what's wrong?" I hear Bash say.

"Your name!" I say, staring at his mother. "Your name is Cornelia?"

"Yes, dear, it's an old name, I know. It's been in our family for generations…"

"No…no…I wrote your name, and I didn't know what it meant. Please, come in. I have so much to tell you."

As they enter, Cornelia turns in a slow circle to examine the house. "I like what you've done with the decor. It is a comfortable home in many ways, but I have had some unnerving experiences here."

"Yes, but I think you've misunderstood what has been happening. Please, will you both come down to my office and let me explain the whole story?"

Bash's face shows concern. No wonder, since the last time he was in my office he saw something that absolutely terrified him.

"Truly, the situation is okay, Bash. Nothing is going to happen. I only went into a trance when I sipped at the elixir I found. Please, follow me and try not to worry.

We enter my office and take a seat. I tread over to my desk and pick up the Ravensdale Manor folder. "Here." I hand it to Bash and open it to show him the manuscript inside. "I need you both to read this. Then, I can help clear it all up."

Bash's tired eyes cling to mine. "What elixir, Sharie?" he questions.

"Remember all the voodoo objects I found?" He nods. "Yeah, well, I left one out." I pad back over to my desk and reach into the drawer to pull out the now empty bottle of absinthe. I hand it over to him.

"I don't understand, luv. What's this?"

"This is the start of it all, Bash. I found this with all the other things. I got curious. With one sip, the first part of the story was written and I don't even remember writing it." Bash and his mother look as though they've gone into shock.

"Oh, my dear." Cornelia says in disquiet. "You drank that old stuff?"

"Sharie, have you gone mad? What if it had been poisonous?!" Bash shouts.

"It's not...or wasn't. I'm fine, obviously—no need for hysterics!" I sit down and take a calming breath. "Did either of you know Prudence was a healer rather than a witch? She and her sister were the original creators of absinthe. And yes, Cornelia, you heard her here in this house. She was murdered for the recipe for this stuff, the true recipe, not for being a witch. That was a sham contrived to turn the people in the parish against her." I put my hand on the manuscript. "Please, both of you, read this. Prudence passed the story through me, herself, but only when I was under the influence of the absinthe. I have tried what they serve now as the modern version of absinthe, and it does not have the same effect."

I watch as both of them read. Every now and then, Bash looks up from the pages in wonderment. Cornelia, on the other hand, looks uncomfortable and is having a harder time, it seems, learning about her ancestor. When they are just about finished, I hear my sister, brother–in-law, and their kids trample through the house. I excuse myself and bolt up the steps to my kitchen.

"Hey, guys. Thanks for coming over."

"We're family," Jack says. "You're not going through this alone."

Charlotte, stumbling behind with bags of food, enters my kitchen. "How's it going so far?"

"Okay…I think." I wrinkle my nose. "Bash seems intrigued, but wary. I'm pretty sure he believes me, but he still thinks I'm in danger. He keeps watching me like I'm going to turn into a monster. His mother is having a harder time swallowing it all down." All at once, we hear a shriek come from my office. We all go running down to find Cornelia standing with her hands up to her face, shaking.

"Mother, what's wrong? What is it?"

"Right here," she points at words on the paper. "she has written the very words I used to hear." Cornelia is turning white and looks faint. "She's telling the truth!" She points to me. "These words I heard for years…I…I would hear my name, then it would be followed by *chene*, *grand chene*, and…*collier*! How could you know? When did you write this, Sharie?"

I take the paper from Cornelia's shaky hand. "This is a break in the flow of the story. I believe it happened when Bash touched me when I was in the trance. That's why your name shocked me when Bash introduced you. I know now

129

that chene and collier refer to the big oak outside and the necklace, but I had no clue who Cornelia was. Now I do." I glance back at Bash. "Bash, Prudence knew you were here that night." I have a sudden epiphany. "When you touched me, she must have said those words and I typed it out!"

Everyone just stands frozen in place. My niece Jaqueline turns toward the window and waves. "Hi, Prudence," she calls out happily.

CHAPTER FOURTEEN

Cornelia's eyes grow terrifyingly big and dart to Jaqueline. I notice, now, they are almost as blue as her son's.

"That child sees her...is it possible?"

Jaqueline turns to us and we both nod. Jack runs to get Cornelia a glass of cold water. "It's true," I say. "My niece can see her. She told me months ago. Now, everyone knows. The dog, Friedo, can see her, too. It's because they have innocent hearts, as Brandy would say."

"Brandy?" Bash questions. "Is that the lady from the voodoo shop we visited?"

"Herbal shop," I correct him. "Yes."

"And she knows all this, too?" Bash sounds exhausted.

I nod. "Yeah, she's a descendant of Lisette Auberjean, Prudence's au pair. That's why I needed to go talk to her. I believe Lisette has written some of the entries in the notebook I found. And she is mentioned in the story Prudence has given me.

Cornelia is still glaring at Jaqueline. "The child can see her!" she repeats, astonished. "Tell me, dear, can you hear her, too?" Jaqueline shakes her head "no."

"She told us it sounds like a buzzing when Prudence tries to speak."

"Mother, do you hear her at all, now?" Bash questions.

"No, nothing, I don't even feel her like I used to."

"Jaqueline, what is Prudence doing right now?" my sister asks.

"Just standing there. She's not even looking at us, just staring out the window."

Bash turns abruptly, eyeing me. "Bash, stop gawking at me like I'm going to turn into a monster. I told you, she is channeled through me, but only when I drink the absinthe. That one, there." I point. "And it's gone. This one had a secret ingredient that no one seems to know about. I'm fine, really I am."

Bash slowly steps over to embrace me. "I'm not scared about that. I'm very worried about your safety. Do we all really know what we're dealing with? I mean, we are talking about an entity, voodoo, supernatural communication. I don't have a clue about any of this. How can I protect you? What if something were to happen, Sharie? I've just found you. I couldn't bear it if something bad happened to you."

Jaqueline tugs on his jeans. "Bash, Aunt Shree isn't in danger. Prudence is sad, not scary. And Friedo likes her, too!"

132

Bash's blue eyes peek at my niece, and he bends on his knee to get down to her level. "I don't want anything to happen to you, or your family, or your Aunt Shree. I just want to know why this is happening."

"She's not going to hurt us, Bash." Jaqueline whispers. "She's smiling, but she is sad. She wants us to follow her."

"Probably along the path to the big oak," I suggest.

Bash stands, gives me a quick kiss on my cheek, and turns towards my brother-in-law. "Jack, you seem calm, yet your daughter can see a spirit. Please, tell me what you make of all this."

"Honestly, Bash, I have concerns. I grew up around these parts. Most around here can or claim to see apparitions. Now, do I believe most actually do? No, probably not. But I have known Charlotte and Sharie for seventeen years. I know to trust their judgment. We are family. So far, there has been no danger. From what I'm gathering and what I've heard about over the years, if the spirit of Prudence Henriod Ravensdale is here, there is a reason."

"Help," I chime in. "She needs our help, but I'm not sure with what, yet. I'm hoping when Brandy comes tomorrow she can give us some answers."

"Brandy?" Bash interrupts. "She's coming here?"

"Yes, she told me to call her if I needed her, and...well...I do. I want to bring her out to the path and the tree where Prudence was murdered. Maybe she can give us more insight."

"Show me where this is," Cornelia pipes in. Her peachy complexion is coming back to her cheeks, and she seems calmer.

"Mother, are you sure you're up to walking?"

"Yes, I'm fine. You don't know what a relief it has been for me to hear this. When I used to visit this house and hear the voice, most of the family thought it was an evil spirit trying to hex us. It caused many fights between my husband and me. But, Sharie, you have taken a step further to figure out a mystery that has troubled descendants of our family for generations. You're a brave soul. We are not cursed after all. Please, Sharie, take me to that place. I want to see it."

We all go outside except Charlotte. I turn to my nephew, who has remained very quiet so far but seems intrigued. "Charlie, you don't have to go. You can stay here with your mom and help her cook us up some brunch, if you want. It's fine if you don't come."

"I'm okay, Aunt Sharie. I want to help. Grandpa always told me my job as a big brother was to protect my little sister. And...well...if she can see this ghost, then maybe Grandpa and Grandma can see us. I want to make them proud."

Jack pats his son on the back. "That is admirable, son. I know how much you miss them. I'm sure they are watching and being guardian angels for us all."

Charlie takes his sister's hand and starts towards the trail. I smile at Charlotte, who's standing in the doorway, beaming with pride. She hands me Friedo's leash.

"You're raising awesome kids, sis, you know that?" I tell her with a smile.

She nods. "Go, get going." She shoos at me. "I'm going to cook us a nice meal. You'll be hungry after your little hike."

"Good. See you in about an hour."

When we get to the tree, Jaqueline lets go of her brother's hand and runs to the bush next to the huge oak. "She was just here! I saw her. She's pointing here."

Cornelia wanders around the area. "I can't believe what happened here so long ago. It's all so sad. But, why does Prudence bring us here? And why does she keep saying collier, or necklace?"

"That is the million-dollar question," I answer. "It's why I have asked for Brandy's help. I'm out of the elixir, the absinthe, so Prudence hasn't given me anything more. But there is something here she needs us to know. I feel it.

"FRIEDO, NO!!!" Charlie yells at the dog. Startled, we all look as the pup is franticly digging under the bush. "No, Friedo! No digging. Bad dog!" Charlie grabs for the dog. "Mom's gonna kill us if he gets too dirty."

Jack laughs. "Yeah, that dog gets more baths than the kids do."

Bash walks over to where Friedo had been digging. "Do you suppose something is here?" He searches the area as we walk over to the same place. Jack and Bash move twigs and branches, and berries drop to the ground. "Keep the dog away, Bash says. "I don't know what kind of berries these are, but I wouldn't want Friedo to eat them. They may be poisonous."

"True," Cornelia agrees. "Might make the poor thing sick. Can never be too careful. Though, it does have rather pretty purple flowers on it."

I nod and smile at her. "I thought the same thing the first time I came out here"

The guys finally walk away from the bush, dusting off their hands. "I don't see anything unusual," Bash comments. "You, Jack?"

"No…but, what are we looking for is the question."

"Jaqueline," I ask, "is Prudence still here? Is she watching us?"

My niece searches around. "No, she left. But, before that she was nodding her head up and down and wiping tears from her face—like this." We all watch as Jaqueline imitates what she saw.

Cornelia steps closer to the tree and closes her eyes. "I don't hear her. I haven't since I've been back. Now, I think I miss it. I should have paid closer attention. I shouldn't have been afraid."

"There was no way you could have known," I reassure her.

For a moment, we are all quiet. Maybe, if we concentrate, she will return. I unfold a sheet of paper, a printout of the part of Prudence's tale that described the night she died. I read it aloud and we trace the steps, trying to see if we can spot a clue of some sort. Over and over, we go through it.

Finally, Charlie asks a question only a ten-year-old who's into zombies would ask. "Aunt Sharie, where did her body go? You said they hung her from this tree. If so, where did she go?"

We all look at each other, dumbfounded over the morbid but excellent question. "I don't really know, Charlie," I say. "I would have to presume, since she was wrongly accused of being a witch and hung for it, the local mortician of that time came and took her body somewhere and buried it, like in a pauper's grave." I look to Jack for helpful insight about my assumption.

"That sounds about right," he decides, shrugging to his son.

"She had no one left?" Charlie asks. "No wonder she's sad. At least with Grandpa and Grandma, we were there to say goodbye. And we know where they are."

"Yes, son, it is sad."

Bash takes my hand. "All those times at the hall of records, there was nothing mentioned of this?"

"Nothing." I shrug. "Just that her cause of death was unknown."

"I think it's enough for today," Jack says. "Let's get back to the house."

We all agree and start to make our way back, following the path. We arrive to see Charlotte out in the courtyard, waving at us. "Just in time!" she shouts. "I just got brunch on the table!"

We all get cleaned up and head for the dining room. My sister puts out a spread of food. Fried chicken, a huge pot of crawfish gumbo over dirty rice, a fresh salad, jalapeno corn bread, and buttery popovers. "Holy crap, Charlotte, you think that's enough food?" I joke.

"It's what I do, and I seem to cook more when I'm nervous," she says, putting a hand to her heart. "Now, come on, everyone—chow time!"

We take our seats, and everyone passes the savory foods around the table. "So, tell me, Cornelia," Charlotte asks, "What did you think of the tree?"

Cornelia dabs at her mouth with her napkin. "First, let me say this food is exquisite, Charlotte. Just wonderful. Now, in all my years of coming here, I don't believe I've ever taken a hike down that path. I don't believe I ever noticed it. Have you, Sebastian?"

"Well, as a boy I ventured into those woods, but that path is way out to the left of the property line, not far from the road. I never went that way. I must say, it's amazing the way you found out about it, Sharie. All so mysterious."

"It is fascinating, isn't it?" Jack chimes in, and we all agree.

"When Brandy comes tomorrow night, I hope she can tell me more or feel something. I mentioned to her on the phone that I was all out of the absinthe. Unfortunately, I can't seem to channel Prudence without it, but I know there is more to the whole bizarre and sad story."

***

My sister and I clean up after brunch with Cornelia's help while the men take the kids out back to play ball. Cornelia tells us stories of Sebastian growing up and some of the trouble a young boy gets into.

Charlotte agrees. "Mom used to say girls don't become a handful until we're teenagers."

"Yeah, I agree, sis. I think that's about the time Daddy started to get grey hair!" We all laugh.

"We were a handful, I think," Charlotte says.

"Oh, I don't know. We could have been worse. We were pretty good students, not on drugs…"

"Ha, at least none they found out about!" Charlotte cuts in.

"We just experimented a little. Dad would have killed us, for sure."

"Oh, you girls remind me of my friends. Just because I was in England didn't mean we didn't do the same things. And, back in my day, it was the mid-sixties. I was away at university and doing some experimenting, myself. But, soon I met Sebastian's father and fell in love, and the rest is history…literally," she says, putting up her arms and turning around to indicate our surroundings.

We all laugh as I reach for a bottle of wine to open. "You girls in?" I say lifting the bottle.

"I'll get the glasses," Charlotte offers.

We pour some wine and make a toast. "I'm glad you came with Sebastian. We had a big fight last week. He was so scared."

"Yes, he did tell me. I suppose I should have told him about things, but I feared he wouldn't have believed me, like his father." She puts her hand over mine. "Sharie, my son loves you very much. Yes, he was distraught about what he saw here that night, but I could tell he was out of his mind with worry about you. He didn't know how he could protect you from all this...I think he feels somewhat helpless, but even so, I know my son will do everything in his power to not let any harm come your way."

"I think I knew he felt that way, but he has got to trust my judgment more."

"I think he does, now, dear," she says, patting my hand. "Just give him time."

A few glasses of wine later, Cornelia seems to be getting tired. She is looking out the window as the spring sky is turning a dusky blue. I step over to her and peer out the window, too. Bash, Jack, and the kids are tossing a tennis ball around the yard while Friedo chases after them and the ball. "You've had a big day, Cornelia. How you doing?" I ask with a semi-smile.

She takes a deep breath and lets it out with a sigh. "I have had an exceptional day, dear," she chuckles. "I *am* tired. Information overload, a great meal, and jet lag, I suppose. I will probably sleep all day, tomorrow."

I glance again out the window and watch Bash having fun running around. "Bash seems energetic."

"He's accustomed to flying. I haven't made this trip in years. I'm going to ask him to call our driver to pick me up soon. You both have some catching up to do." She gives me a wink. My eyes go wide, and I feel my cheeks go hot. Cornelia laughs. "Oh, my dear, I wasn't born yesterday.

140

Isn't it fascinating how two people can find each other and fall in love in the most mysterious ways?"

"I'm glad I got to meet you, Cornelia, even under these circumstances. We are all involved in a unique situation. I intend to get to the bottom of it."

"Of that, I have no doubt," she says. "I am looking forward to reading the book when it's all finished."

"You and Bash will be the first to get shiny, new copies. I will definitely be mentioning you both in the dedications, of course."

Cornelia reaches to give me a hug. It feels good, just like a motherly one should, and I suddenly miss my mom.

Bash walks in and interrupts. "Nice to see my two favorite girls hugging it out," he says with a smug grin.

"She's a wonderful girl, Sebastian, and she has a wonderful family. Now, it would please me to get out of everyone's way and get some rest. Could you please call the driver for me so you and Sharie can be alone to talk and make up properly?" she winks.

CHAPTER FIFTEEN

Everyone has gone but Bash. I go out on my porch for some air with a glass of wine. It's quiet. I hear only crickets and see an occasional firefly. A vivid, full moon is keeping everything bright. I feel as though a heavy weight has been lifted from my shoulders. Suddenly, I am bombarded with thoughts of the day's events. In my head, ideas and passages finally unfold, spinning a story to blend with the one Prudence has given me. Finally, my own creativity has awakened and is running wild. Keeping all that burden on myself had been stifling, but I now have support.

Bash comes out to join me, and the slam of the screen door snaps me out of my thoughts. I stand as he comes towards me. "What are you doing out here, luv?"

I hold up a finger and hand him my wineglass. "Shh...I need to get my notebook." Spinning on my heel, I dart into the house. Bash follows right behind me.

"What is it? What's wrong?"

"Nothing!" I say, grinning wide. "I have some ideas I need to write down before I forget them." I scribble frantically and whisper to myself. When I finish, I look up. Bash is still holding my wineglass, but now it's empty. He is smiling at me. "What?" I ask him.

"You. You are amazing. With all that has happened. You are such a strong woman, Sharie. I don't deserve you."

Without a word, I move a few steps in his direction. I take the empty wineglass from his fingers and place it on the coffee table. I examine his face, taking in all his masculinity. His brown, floppy curls, piercing sapphire eyes, strong jawline, and lips that burn me deep down with his kisses. He puts his hands on my waist and gazes back at me. "Mr. Devonshire, are you going to make me wait all night, or are you going to kiss me?"

He seals his lips to mine, and slowly our tongues mingle together. I move my hands to his chest. I can feel his heart beating strong. My breath hitches as he follows the length of my body with his touch. His kisses trail down the side of my neck and to my collar bone. My knees instantly go weak. My head spins. Automatically, a throb between my legs is stirred by his kiss alone. *I need this man inside me.* My hips nudge forward, and Bash presses me against him. I run my hand down his chest and slightly into the waistband of his loose jeans for a moment before I unbutton them.

"I can't wait to feel your legs wrapped around my waist as I sink in to you," he growls.

Nearly bursting from the heavy pressure of arousal, I jump up, swinging my legs around him. Bash catches me and holds me to him as I lift my shirt off. We fall onto the sofa. Bash stands to slip off my pants then hurriedly remove his own.

Tearing open a condom, he glances at me. "Do you want to go upstairs?"

"I won't make it," I say, panting hard. "Now, Bash. I want you now!"

He starts at my feet, taking hold of each one, and slowly spreads my legs. Kneeling between them, he lowers his head and kisses up my thigh and over to my hip, across to my belly button, and trails his tongue all the way down till he finds me, open and needing his touch. He drives me crazy with his mouth till I can't take any more. I twist my fingers in his hair and beg for him…"Bash! I loudly moan his name. Slowly, he eases his way back up to my breasts and neck, and when our eyes lock on to each other, he slips himself inside me. We both moan with pleasure, my legs secure around him as he pounds into me. I meet every thrust with my hips, our bodies sleek with sweet sweat. It's not long before the orgasm is ready to take me. My fingers dig into his back as my body tightens.

He searches my face, his eyes like blue fire as he whispers, "Come with me, luv." All at once, on his command, we shatter with a force so strong we lose our breath. Bash moans deep from his throat and collapses on top of me with his head on my chest. I can feel both our hearts hammering so fast they might burst.

We stay embraced till it all subsides. Bash gets up and pads to the kitchen then returns with two bottles of water. He grabs the blanket from the end of the sofa and wraps me in it.

"Here, drink some water. That was one hell of a workout. I am completely drained."

"I'll say it was. My throat is dry, and my legs are weak."

"What do you say I help you to bed and we relax a bit before I make you scream my name again," he says with a smirk.

I feel myself turn bright red. "I didn't scream your name."

"What's this? Getting bashful on me again?" He chuckles. Lifting my chin with his fingers so he can see right into my eyes, he says, "I love you, Sharie. I love making love to you. And, if you ever *stop* screaming my name, it will kill me." He stands, scooping me up in his arms and carrying me up the stairs to bed.

***

I wake to the smell of coffee brewing. The sun is up and bright. I realize I've slept late and glance at my phone to find it's nearly eight-thirty. "Bash?" I call out.

"Be up in a minute, luv—bringing you coffee."

In a few minutes, he enters the bedroom, completely naked, with a mug of coffee in each hand. The sight of this makes me grin.

"Ah, smiles from my lady," he says as he hands me a steaming cup of Java. "Every man should see a smile like that on a Monday morning," he adds, crawling back into bed with me. "You look happy and well satisfied. I assume I have satiated your every desire with the utmost pleasure?"

I raise my eyebrows and smile wider. "*You* are the *man*," I tell him with a nod. "But, truthfully, I was really smiling at you, naked, with coffee mugs in your hands. That made my morning, right there." He gives me his charming smirk and starts to scroll and text on his phone.

"It's Monday," I say. "Don't you always have a busy, crazy day on Mondays?"

"Yes, but I have cleared my schedule for a few days, Sharie. I have people who fill me in on things. I don't have to be anywhere but right here."

I cock my head to the side, squinting at him through my lashes. "You're not going to leave me alone today, are you?" I tease, my tone slightly sarcastic.

"No," he replies, still tapping away on his phone, not missing a beat.

"But, I have work to do," I continue. "I intend to write. I have to work with those ideas I jotted down last night. So I will be busy most of the day."

"Fine with me, luv. I brought my laptop along. We both can do some work, but I'm not leaving you home alone for long hours of the day."

Happy but somewhat confused, I sense he is still trying to make up for leaving me. "Bash, what do you think is going to happen?"

His texting finished, he tosses his phone down on the bed. "I just want to be here for you, just in case you need my help."

"Hmm…or maybe you think I'll need saving."

"What do you want me to say, Sharie? Please, I just need to be here, where you are. And…yes, in case you come into a problem."

"What about your mother? You're going to leave her alone all day?"

"Mother will probably sleep most of the day away. I will have a car sent to pick her up later and deliver her here, along with dinner."

My mouth must have been open, because he shuts it with the tips of his fingers under my chin. I roll my eyes. "You can't be serious." He squirms closer to me and puts his baby blues inches from my face. "Don't be snarky, luv," he hisses. "What do you say, before we start our day, we go for number four?"

I bunch my eyebrows together. "Number four?" I question.

"Yes, luv," he says, flashing me a toothy grin. "I made you yell my name three times last night. I desperately need to hear it again."

***

All day long, I am busy at work, adding to my manuscript. Bash taps away at his laptop. When he needs to take a call, he steps out to talk so he doesn't disturb me. He brings me water or tea and even makes me stop for lunch.

As the day moves forward, I manage to get a lot accomplished. Every now and then, I can feel a pause in my atmosphere. Glancing up over my computer screen to where Bash is sitting and using my little coffee table as his desk, I see him watching me with a small, content smile. At times, we share loving glances. Bash makes me feel protected, warm, loved. *I could get used to this.*

Around six p.m., I lean back in my seat, drinking the last sip of my tea that has now gone cold. I rub at my eyes.

"I think we should call it a day, luv. Mother and dinner will be arriving in an hour. What time did you say Brandy was to be here?"

I stretch my back and yawn. "After she closes the shop. She told me she would get here by nine."

Bash makes his way over to me and takes my hands, coaxing me out of the chair. He wraps me in his embrace, kisses me slow and with longing. When he breaks the kiss, his face is serious. "I have been waiting all day to do that," he murmurs.

I move a curl off his forehead and put my arms around his neck. "Do it again," I whisper.

"Ms. Donovan! On the pull, I see," he says through that smirk I love.

"I'm not familiar with your English slang, Mr. Devonshire, but if it means you're going to kiss me again, then just shut up and do it."

"Close." He smiles wider and lifts his brows up and down. "Maybe a little more than a kiss…"

***

Dinner with Bash and his mother is enjoyable. He had placed an order with a local caterer who delivered us a superb gourmet meal of poached salmon in white wine with dill and capers. It also includes a fresh vegetable mix, rice pilaf, and two excellent bottles of white wine as well as bread pudding with a whiskey sauce for dessert.

It is so good, I can't believe it. "Where did you find these guys?" I question.

Bash opens one of the wine bottles and pours me and his mother each a glass. "Found them years ago," he says. "Sometimes I need to entertain clients at the penthouse when the cook is off. So, I placed a call had it brought here, this time. They know what I like, and I am getting to know what you like," he added with a smug smile.

"This is very good," Cornelia says, wiping her mouth daintily, "but your sister cooks very well, too. You must take me to her restaurant while I'm here."

I nod with a smile. "Charlotte would love that. She loves cooking for people and making a fuss."

"She does, indeed," Bash agreed.

Cornelia eyes me for a minute. "I must read some of your books, Sharie. Sebastian tells me they are fun and full of mystery, and...sex!"

I choke on my wine, and Bash hands me my napkin. "You all right, luv?"

"Uh...yeah..." I say, clearing my throat. "I write mystery-romance, contemporary stuff. Nothing too smutty."

"I will have to check them out, dear. I love a good read, and smutty isn't so bad, you know."

"Okay, then. Maybe I will smutty up the next one." I toss my wide eyes toward Bash. He smiles tightly, and I

149

change the subject. "Uh, so, Cornelia, I'm glad you're here. You will get a chance to meet Brandy. She has this book of her family tree. She is a descendant of Lisette Auberjean, Prudence's au pair.

"Yes, I remember reading about Lisette in your manuscript. It is all very different than the story that has been handed down. We thought they were some kind of coven. It's all so sad to think about what really happened all those years ago. Do you believe Brandy can help figure out the rest?"

"I'm counting on it," I said, sitting back in my chair, my belly full of food.

Bash clears his throat and reaches for more wine. "Well I, for one, am not looking forward to it. But, I do want some closure for you…for Mum, for us. I feel helpless with this whole bloody thing. I'm accustomed to control and to having answers. I don't like the in-between."

"Just like your father. You can't control everything, Sebastian," his mother scolds with a pitched eyebrow.

I reach over and place my hand on top of Bash's. "We are going to get closure. We all will be fine. Stop worrying, Bash."

***

Two hours later and spot on time, my doorbell rings. I open the door to Brandy, who is standing there with a very old woman beside her. They both smile at me as we exchange pleasantries and I invite them in. "Sharie, this is a

150

very close friend and colleague of my grandmother's and my mother's. This is Miss Ophelia Mavis. She is one hundred and one years old. When I told my mother about you, she called Miss Ophelia, who then wanted to come and see you and talk with you, herself."

"Hello, Miss Ophelia. It's very nice to meet you," I say, getting a strange twinge in my stomach. Nerves, I think. I show them to the sitting room and introduce everyone who hasn't already met. "Please, everyone, have a seat. Can I get anything for anybody? Water, tea, wine?"

"Oh, a cup of tea would be lovely," Ophelia says, and I detect that her slight Southern accent also has hints of the Carribbean.

Bash turns on his heal. "Tea, coming up. I will be happy to get that. Mother, tea for you as well?"

"Yes, Sebastian. Thank you."

I sit down next to Brandy. Ophelia is looking around the room with a pleasant smile on her face. She's small and is wearing a wig of silver curls. Like Brandy, she has a mocha-cream complexion, but Ophelia's is littered with lines and age spots. Her eyes look like they were once blue but are so old they now have a milky film covering them. Cataracts, I guess.

Noting her interest in the surroundings, I say to Ophelia, "I bought this house from Mrs. Devonshire and Sebastian. Tell me, Miss Ophelia, what has brought you to see me this evening?"

Ophelia's head turns in my direction, but her eyes do not focus on me. I notice she looks at me more with her peripheral vision, not straight on.

"Brandy, here, tells me you have been chosen. By way of the absinthe, Prudence Henriod Ravensdale has chosen to tell her story through you. I, too, know a thing or two about it. How evil the people and how cruel the times were, all dem years ago. My family knew the Auberjeans, and I have stories of my own to tell. Ms. Donovan, do you know your family tree at all?"

"Not too far back." I shrug a shoulder.

Ophelia closes those opaque, old eyes and breathes in deep. "All dem years ago"—she shakes her head, letting out an exhalation—"some of the Irish settlers came south, looking for work. Sadly, nothing paid too well, at least not as well as being a thug. Sometimes, some folk gotta do what they need to do to survive.

"It was a hard life in dem days. A big name here at the time was Donovan. Eli Fitzgerald Donovan. A tall, brown-haired, muscular man they say he was. Wasn't cut out to be a thug, but couldn't get work on the docks. They say he did odd jobs for hire, you know, roughin' someone up for money or what have you. Story goes, E. F. Donovan was a friend of Prudence, knew Lisette too. And, some say, he was there the night Prudence died. I believe you are a descendant of dat man."

Chills of ice tingle my spine. My heart thuds hard. Bash interrupts as he comes in with the ladies' tea. "Sharie, luv, can I get you something?"

I slowly turn my head to face him. His usual, smirky smile quickly dissolves as he focuses on me. He knows I'm distraught. Before he can speak, I sputter out, "Wine…a big glass of wine."

CHAPTER SIXTEEN

Turning back to Ophelia, I slide off my seat onto my knees and gently take hold of her hands. I feel my insides start to tremble, my mouth going dry. "Are you telling me this Eli Donovan is a relation of mine? How could you know for sure?"

Brandy interrupts to explain. "Ophelia is the longest-living member of the Daughters of Historical Ancestry. It's a very private and secretive society. Made up of some Catholic priests, voodoo queen high priestesses, and even a few DOCs."

I shake my head. "DOCs?" I question.

"Daughters of the Confederacy," she explains.

My eyes go wide. "Bash!" I call out. "Where are you with my wine?"

"Right here, luv," he says, handing it to me. I take a big mouthful. I am digesting this information in increments. I get the feeling it's not mixing with my dinner.

"Sharie, come sit back on the sofa." Bash helps me to my feet and I sit back on the cushion. His eyes serious, he asks, "Are you all right? Maybe we shouldn't continue."

"I'm fine," I say, my voice raw. Another big sip of wine and I clear my throat. "Miss Ophelia, please continue." I take a big, cleansing breath and give my best tight-lipped smile. I am afraid to hear more but too frightened not to know. I try to relax. I glance at Cornelia, and she seems calm and very intrigued. She takes my hand and tells her son to stop fussing over me and to take a seat. She quickly winks her eye at me. Her gesture is motherly and warm. I stifle a giggle because Bash is taking her advice without question.

"Sharie, after you came to see me at the shop, my mother and Miss Ophelia stopped in to say hello. I told them all about you and what we discussed. Then Miss Ophelia decided to do some checking."

"Yes," Ophelia states with a smile and puts down her tea cup. "There are things—dates and people, strange and mysterious stories—that the hall of records just would not have, one might say, because no one could explain them. My friends and I researched our records and dove into your family ancestry.

"Eli Fitzgerald Donovan, I believe, was your four-times great-grandfather. Story has it, Eli was hired with a bunch of other men to put a scare into others who owed gambling debts, or to collect money for various things. One day, it was Prudence's name that was on the list. Eli wanted no part of this. He told his thug friends Prudence once saved his little girl from the fever. Back then, they didn't have medications like today's, but healers like Prudence and Lisette who knew how to make remedies from God's good

Earth healed the sick or helped them move on, peacefully. Eli told them he would not harm Prudence Ravensdale. Because of this, it put Eli in a bad spot. He got laid off, even though he had a wife and children to feed. He watched from afar as the Ravensdale family broke apart. Once or twice, he even tried to stop those other thugs. Eli was warned to stay out of it or threats would be leveled against his own family.

"According to Lisette, Eli knew what those men had done to Prudence. So Lisette found Eli, and together they took Prudence's body and buried her so no one would find her. Lisette claimed to have put her in a blue velvet sack with things that were dear to her heart. Lisette spoke some prayers at the grave, and she and Eli parted ways. He packed up his family and migrated back north. Documents state he ended up in Delaware and found work in a shipyard. Lived out the rest of his life with his family."

We are all quiet when Ophelia finishes her story. My head is spinning as I put in the missing puzzle pieces. "I am from Maryland," I blurt out, "but I have heard our family settled in Delaware, first. I know nothing of anyone having been here in Louisiana."

"Eli kept that secret, I think, for fear he would be found," Ophelia answers.

My mind now races as fast as my heart. My notes, my manuscript. "Dubied!" I spit out the name, loud. I am a little out of breath from excitement. "Eli moved north to hide from Monsieur Dubied. He is the one who forced Prudence and her sister to sell him their elixir recipe, then realized later they had not given him the exact ingredients. He sent his men over here and hired some more to do his dirty work. They terrorized her…they nearly killed her for that missing ingredient, but she drank a special elixir so she could end her life just before they could violate her and then finish her off! They hung her from the big oak tree on the path in the woods behind the house!"

Cornelia stood abruptly, almost knocking over my wine glass. "Oh God...I hear her!" Cornelia put her hand to her head. "She has spoken my name...and the same words as before: grand chene and collier."

I quickly glance around the room as if I am going to see Prudence. Bash looks stunned but not panicked. Brandy cocks her head a little. "You can hear her, Mrs. Devonshire?"

"Yes, I always have...for years she has been telling me the same thing over and over, but I never had even a clue as to why until I read Sharie's manuscript and walked along that path."

"The oak tree is where you say she was hung?" Ophelia asks.

"Yes, chene is tree and collier is necklace. She keeps telling Cornelia and my niece where she was killed."

Brandy eyes me curiously. "You told me your niece only sees her."

"That is true." I nod. "Jaqueline only sees her but says she is always pointing outside. When we went to the tree, she told us Prudence was pointing to it or the bush that is next to it. But we can't figure out why."

Brandy moves her eyes to Ophelia and back to me. "Does it say anywhere where Prudence's body is buried?"

Seems that is the big question. We all glance at each other, searching for an answer, then most everyone stares in my direction.

"I haven't gotten any more of the story from Prudence. I am out of her absinthe." I almost feel as if I have let her down. I sit back. Cornelia takes my hand again, and I turn to her.

"Do you still hear her?" I ask.

"No, dear, she is quiet again."

"It's got to be something with that tree," Bash offers, "but what?"

Brandy's eyes seem far away as she thinks. "How far is the tree from here, Sharie?"

"It's a good hike, almost up to the highway. At any rate, it's too dark to go there, now."

"I need to see it, please."

I toss a glance at Bash. "I have flashlights in the kitchen cupboard. Closest to the back door."

He nods. "Right. I guess we are going on a hike."

I ask Cornelia and Ophelia to stay in the house together. This trek out in the wilderness shouldn't take too long. I hope.

We go out my back door and head for the path. So far, it is all too surreal for me. Like the dream I had. Same kind of night—dewy grass, low fog clinging to the ground, a damp chill in the air. The tiny hairs on the back of my neck keep shivering.

Bash takes the lead while Brandy and I follow behind. I move to his side and hold on to his hand for the duration of the hike. Things can look different at night, and I'm uneasy.

"Don't be afraid," Bash says. "I won't let anything happen to you."

Good to know, I think. *What could happen on a creepy night in the dark in the woods?*

Finally, I hear the far-off sounds of traffic and I know we've made it. A small wave of relief drifts over me, but is it because we've arrived unscathed or because I don't see the skeleton of Prudence wearing a nun's habit?

We direct the beams of light up the trunk of the tree and over across the surrounding area. "This is it," I inform Brandy. "This is where she was beaten and hanged."

Brandy steps gingerly around the tree. She touches the bushy plant, pulls at one of its purple flowers, and inhales its scent. Taking a berry, she mushes it between her fingers. "Belladonna!" she exclaims.

Bash furrows his brows. "Elaborate, please."

"Belladonna is a powerful herb used for a lot of things"—she pauses, raising an eyebrow at me—"with hallucinations being on the top of the list. Dilated eyes, numbing pains. Too much of a dose can be deadly. Some call it nightshade, some call these berries *devil's cherries*."

"Why would that be growing here, of all places? Does that grow wild?" I ask.

Brandy is still and focusing on the plant. "I'm going to find out." She kneels on the ground and opens her big handbag and pulls out a little book and a small mortar and pestle. She places some of the berries in the mortar and smashes them with the pestle. Reaching in her bag of tricks again, she pulls out a little knife. She pricks her finger and allows a few droplets of blood to drip into the mix.

Bash grabs my arm and whispers in my ear, "What the bloody hell is she doing?"

I shrug exaggeratedly, my eyes wide in surprise. I'm freaked out, too. "Let's just see what happens," I whisper back.

Brandy stirs her blood-and-berry mixture then adds a few capfuls of water from a bottle she had also brought out of that magic bag. Taking her finger, she scoops up some of the dark paste and licks it off.

Bash and I recoil at the same time. We watch as she swirls it in her mouth like a fine wine and swallows it down. She starts whispering very low. I can't make out what she is saying, but even if I could I'm sure it wouldn't make any difference. I am clueless about this religion and its rituals.

Still on her knees, Brandy bends forward, putting her ear to the ground. Chanting a whispered plea, she sits back up and scoops up a handful of dirt with each hand. Her chant gets a little louder and more desperate. She tosses the dirt away and takes another finger-full of the mixture and licks it off.

She falls forward, digging the dirt. Her chanting stops suddenly as a wind gust envelopes us like a tiny, gentle tornado. Brandy stands with the dirt in her hands and throws it at the wind. She follows it to the belladonna bush.

Bash and I stand there, silent and mesmerized. In the dark, we shine the glow of our flashlights on Brandy, whose back is to us. She is almost zombie-like in her movements. Kneeling on the ground again, she bends, putting her ear to the cool, dewy grass. Minutes pass. The wind still bellows as Brandy stands and turns toward us. Her eyes are clouded over. I gasp and drop my flashlight. Bash pulls me into his arms as we keep watching. "Very reminiscent of the night I found you looking very much like that." His words make me nauseous. I hold on to him tighter.

All at once the gusts of wind stop. Brandy falls to the ground like a rag doll. We sprint over to help her.

"She's knocked out!" Bash exclaims. He is holding her across his lap.

"Brandy!" I yell her name, tapping her lightly on her cheek. "Brandy, can you hear me?" I grab her bottle from the ground, pour some water onto my hand, and spritz her face with it.

Bash nods at me. "She's coming around."

When Brandy's eyes open, they have returned to the hazel color I remember. "Brandy, are you okay? You passed out. What is happening?"

She sits up, and I hand her the water bottle. "Thanks," she says on an intake of air. She takes a few more deep breaths and sips more water.

"Prudence...is buried right there." Brandy points a dirty finger toward the spot. "Lisette and Eli put her right there, and Lisette came back and planted the belladonna on top of her to mark the grave. Not sure why...but I have some ideas. The biggest problem we have right now is…she wants out."

I flash a piercing gaze at Bash over the top of Brandy's head. He returns the look with questioning eyes.

"What do you mean 'she wants out'?" Bash is not happy. This is more statement than question. Before I can say what I am thinking, Bash beats me to it. "Who the hell is going to dig up a bloody corpse that's been in the ground for almost 200 years?"

Shaking my head, I stand there, perplexed. "Brandy, how do you know this? What did you do?"

"I did an invocation. I had a feeling she was buried here, so I took the berries and offered my blood. I diluted it with water so I could see just enough. Prudence came to me. She is definitely here, and you were right, Sharie; she needs help. As I told you before, she is in a state of unrest. Her request is small: Move her near her family."

"But how? Move her…move her, where?" My voice rises.

"I know where," Bash says calmly while helping Brandy to her feet. "She needs to be taken to Devonshire. On the grounds, we have a family cemetery. That is where she needs to be. Her husband Bernard is buried there, along with their three daughters and their own husbands and families. I never understood why their headstones all said, 'Apart we are, be it centuries, we long to reunite in the hereafter.'" He huffs a laugh. "Now, I know what it means."

I'm quiet, registering all of this in my brain. Brandy tripping out on berries, finding out Prudence is right here. My four-times great-grandfather knew her, even helped bury her. Now, Bash's mention of the headstones. My eyes go a little blurry as tears fill them. "They have been waiting for her…Wife, mother." The tears spill out, running down my cheeks. I can't help it; I am overcome with sadness. Bash pulls me into his embrace and swipes my damp face with a light touch of his fingertips.

"Shhh…luv, we will rectify this. We can have her remains exhumed and taken home to where she needs to be."

We get back to the house, and Cornelia and Ophelia are still sitting where we left them. They both seem to be having a very friendly conversation. As we three approach them, Cornelia takes one look at us and jumps to her feet. "Dear God, are you all right?"

"Yes, Mother, we are fine, but we have some news."

Ophelia puts out her hands, and Brandy reaches for them. "I'm fine, too," she assures the old woman and gives her a hug. "There's a belladonna plant out there. I did an offering invocation. Prudence is buried under the plant, next to the oak tree. I'll tell you about it on the drive home. We should go. I am completely drained, and it's getting late for you."

Cornelia glances from us to them and back.

"We will fill you in," I tell her. "Let me just walk them out." I proceed to the door following Brandy and Ophelia. Brandy has the older lady by the arm to steady her, but Brandy is the one who seems so fragile and weak at the moment. The voodoo mojo she did really must have exhausted her. "Are you sure you can drive? We would be happy to drive you home, if you need the help."

Brandy stands at the door with a ghost of smile as I open it for them. "Thank you, Sharie. It's kind of you to offer, but I will be right as rain in a few moments. It takes a little while to completely recover. I am fine, truly. I will talk with you soon, I'm sure. Call me when you decide to dig. I will be here."

I give her a sad but thankful smile. "Thank you for everything. I feel like I need to pay you, though. Please let me give you something..." I plead.

"Nothing needed." She holds up her long, slender hands. "I am happy to help. Like your man says, we will make this right."

We hug, tight. I feel her sincerity in that embrace and know we are going to be friends forever. "Miss Ophelia, I feel like I owe you a big debt for finding out all you did about my family tree. I just wish my parents were alive to share this wonderful information."

"I was just happy to help," she replies with a kind smile on her wise and knowing face. I hug them both again and help Brandy get Ophelia down the few porch steps. As I watch them get in the car, two strong arms circle me from behind. Bash's touch and his comforting scent calm my nerves.

"Hey, you," I say. He nuzzles my neck then turns me around, putting both hands on my face and tilting my head where he needs it to be so he can give me a proper kiss.

"Hey, you," he echoes. He sighs as his deep, blue eyes take me in. The look of concern on his face makes my stomach quiver. "Feeling better?"

I nod. "I am now, in your arms, safe. I love you, Bash."

He gives me his crooked smirk. "I was hoping you would say that." He leans in for another kiss, holding me tight against him. I pull away abruptly. "We have to tell your mother what happened."

"I already did," he says, pulling me back in. "She's getting ready to leave. The car will be here for her in a few minutes."

I give Bash a quick kiss and take his hand. We both walk in to say good night to his mother.

In the kitchen, Cornelia is cleaning up the tea mugs and wiping down the counter. She seems a bit out of sorts and nervous. "Cornelia?" I murmur, watching her clean with force. "You don't have to clean up. Is everything okay?" She ignores me.

Bash leans on the counter, gently stopping his mother's hand. "Mother—Sharie is talking to you," he says, his voice slightly stern.

"Bash, it's okay," I say, putting my own hand on his arm to move it out of her way. I step over to Cornelia and reach for the sponge in her hand. "Cornelia, really, you don't have to do this."

She drops the sponge. "I need to do something…normal," she stutters out as she gazes at us. "Just normal. Nothing here is ever normal. What happens now? If we move her to the family cemetery, does it stop, Sharie?" She grabs my forearms, her fingers cold. I can feel her shake. "Will Prudence go quiet? Will it be over?"

I move my eyes to Bash. He uncrosses his arms from his chest and strides around the counter. "Mother, calm down.

We will handle it. You don't have to be involved anymore, if you don't want to be."

"That's right." I nod, looking back at her with compassion. She's so petite and delicate. "Bash and I will fix things. Then, she will be at rest and won't need our help any longer."

Cornelia's intense, blue gaze settles on mine. "You are so strong, Sharie. How do you handle all this?" She turns her head to Bash then back to me. "My son is lucky he's found you. And—the way it all has come about. It's so unbelievably profound."

Bash's cell phone beeps, and he checks the screen. "Mother, your car is waiting. Get some sleep. Tomorrow you could go shopping or just sit on the dock and relax. Please, don't worry."

We escort her to the door. She hugs me and says good night. Bash walks with her to the car, says a couple of words to the driver, then comes back inside the house.

"I need a hot shower," I say to him, feeling mentally drained.

"Go on up, luv. I'll lock up."

I reach out my hand to touch his masculine, chiseled face. He has a little more than a five-o'clock shadow. I smile. "Your mother got it wrong, you know…I am the lucky one. She thinks I am strong, but I am getting some of that strength from you. I thought I was doing just fine on my own, but now I realize…having you here with me makes all this more bearable."

"Sharie," Bash breathes my name as he pulls me toward him. "You are the strongest, bravest woman I have ever come across. You, my love, are amazing—with or without me. I will always be in your corner. Remember that, Sharie." Our eyes lock for an instant before he gives me a chaste kiss on the top of my nose and spins me around to face the stairs. "Go take your shower," he commands and gives me a tap on my ass. "I'll be right up."

CHAPTER SEVENTEEN

I place my hands on the tile beneath the shower spray, letting the hot water run down to my head and face then over my shoulders and back. It feels so good, I honestly could melt. I hear the click of the shower door, and suddenly the same strong arms are surrounding me again, pulling me away from the wall and leaning me back against a muscular chest.

Bash's hands start to soap and caress my body while he nibbles on my neck. I feel his erection up against my hip, and I reach back and tenderly stroke him. He hisses in my ear, and it causes a flurry of chills to scatter across my wet skin. His hand goes between my legs and his fingers caress the most tender spot, causing my knees to go weak.

After the evening we've just had, it feels so good to be in a pair of strong arms, making love, gratifying each other's wants and needs. I turn and seal my mouth to his, and he gently pushes me against the shower wall, coaxing me to wrap my legs around him. With his help, I do.

He pins me against the wall with his hard body, balancing me with his hands securely on my ass as the hot, steamy water rains over us from above. He kisses my breasts and, in one swift move, pushes into me. His hips thrust and thrust. My fingers dig into his shoulders as I bounce up and down.

The muscles in my stomach tighten and my toes curl as the fervent buildup reaches its apex and starts to erupt. Like a wave crashing over me, the orgasm robs me of breath, my head goes back as a blissful wail escapes from my throat. Bash continues to pump until I ride it out. He follows and finishes in three abrupt thrusts, filling me up with a trembling groan.

Gently, he helps me back onto my feet and we collapse to the shower floor. I am out of breath and my legs are shaky. We just stare at each other. Bash lifts a finger to my face and traces along my cheek and lips, kissing me tenderly. "Like I said, you're amazing."

***

Slivers of sunlight find us still in bed, spooning. I stir slightly, making Bash moan, "No, let's sleep in a little longer."

I roll over to face him. "I have research to do and maybe some calls to make," I say with slight elation. "Who does one call to exhume a body? Or do we do it ourselves?"

Bash props himself up on his elbow, rubbing a hand through his mop of curls and exposing a pointed eyebrow. He needs a shave and a haircut, but I think I like him better scruffy. With his face still puffy from sleep, he is adorable.

"What are you going on about, luv? Calling who to do what?"

I sit up straighter. "We need to call someone to dig up and move Prudence. Or, should we not say anything, just do it ourselves? I was thinking last night...I am guessing we would have to call the local medical examiner, you know, like forensics/CSI stuff. But that would make police and reporters come around. Also, I would have to guess there are permits and lots of red tape involved. I'm scared we would not get to do what is needed...who would believe it? No...I suggest we do it ourselves."

Bash sits up and stumbles out of bed, grabbing a pair of boxers and slipping them on.

"Where you going?" I ask him.

He turns back to me, lips pursed. "If we are going to go on with this morbid conversation, I need coffee and food, first."

**

Sitting with our coffee and PB&J toast, Bash and I talk over our options. We both agree about not wanting to have reporters, cops, and God knows who else coming out making a big spectacle. We also surmise that exposing our involvement with the supernatural might not be beneficial to our personal and professional lives. And, would it help or hinder the sale of my book to tout it as a true story? After going round and round, we sit quietly, nibbling breakfast, letting all the information soak in. I can see the wheels in his head spinning. The look of severe concentration on his face makes me giggle.

Bash blinks, doing a double-take at me. "What are you laughing about?"

"I don't know," I answer with a shrug. "Your face is so serious, it makes me laugh to see you with such intensity. It's kind of sexy." He rolls his eyes and shakes his head with a chuckle.

"Listen," I continue, "I still say we should go for it…dig her up ourselves."

Bash winces at my suggestion. "I'm going to make a call to get some information," he says. "I think you should also call your sister and Jack. You need to let them know what's going on."

"I agree. In fact, my sister is probably waiting by the phone. I will make it a point to tell gossipy Gertie not to open her mouth."

"Good idea, luv," he says with a light tap on the tip of my nose before swiftly picking up our plates and taking them to the sink.

I watch him as he cleans up and loads the dishwasher—his muscular arms flexing and his toned abs rippling in the morning sun that's shining through the kitchen window. *What a sight to behold*, I shamelessly think to myself. Sebastian's body is flawless, not overly muscled but trim and cut to perfection.

He glances up at me. "Am I doing something wrong?"

I smile seductively. "Oh, no…you're doing everything right."

***

An hour after we've made love yet again—or as Bash calls it, giving my lady parts a proper jostling—he is dressed and headed to his condo to change into a suit for a big shareholders' conference he just could not avoid. "I'm sorry I have to leave you, but this is out of my hands. I must attend this dreadful meeting. I will see you for dinner." Reaching for me, he plants a hot kiss over my mouth then pauses to take a moment to just look at me. "Love you, Sharie. See you soon."

I wave goodbye to Bash from the front porch as he drives off. Feeling suddenly too much like a housewife, I smile and let out a big sigh. I head down to my office with my cell phone to call Charlotte.

I begin to fill her in on what has transpired and how Prudence needs to be relocated and laid to rest with her family in Devonshire.

"Who or how does one go about doing this?" Charlotte asks. I laugh and tell her I said the same exact words to Bash this morning.

"I'm not too sure about who…I can guess how. Do me a favor, Charlotte, and don't open your mouth about this, not to anyone. The last thing we need is reporters snooping around. I'd like to do this on our own, if we can."

"Well Jesus, Sharie, who would I tell? I haven't told anyone anything so far."

"Okay, then let's keep it that way, because sometimes, Char, you can have diarrhea of the mouth; you trust too many people."

"HEY!" she squeals. "I do not!

"Oh yeah? Tell me," I question her, my voice dripping with suspicion, "how many people in your restaurant know Bash and I became a couple, then had a lover's quarrel, and now are back together?"

"That's different," she coos. "It's just everyday gossip. This whole spirit-from-beyond business—my daughter, you and the drink, Brandy and her voodoo—this is not something we can just talk about, especially in the South. People here are wary of such things. I'm still floored about finding out about our four-times great-grandfather. That's so exciting!"

"Yeah, I agree. Hey, I was thinking, Charlotte, that when all this is over and the dust settles, we should have a family-tree book made of our own. Something we can pass on through generations."

"That's a great idea, Sharie. I think our kids will enjoy that."

I raise my eyebrows at her statement and my hand is starting to perspire on to my smartphone. "*Our* kids?" I ask tightly.

I hear her smug laughter come through the phone. "Yes, Sharie. Jack and I both see it coming. Bash is the one. I feel it in my bones."

I quickly change the subject. "Speaking of bones, we should all get together for a family dinner soon. Help me figure out what to do about Prudence.

"Sounds good. I'll talk to Jack and see what he thinks. Call you later?"

"Yep. Thanks, Charlotte. Love you."

"Awww…love you, too, baby sis. You'll see—it will all be fine. We'll get her moved and at rest. Your book will get done, and hopefully there will be a wedding in our future!"

I squeeze the phone, pretending it's her neck.

"Shut up," I blurt. My sister loves to push. She knows it aggravates me, so she's all about antagonizing. Sibling love. I hear her evil laugh mocking me.

"Don't be such a bitch, Sharie. I'm just joking…a little. Hello? Did you hang up?"

"No, but I'm about to."

"Ugh. Fine, I'll stop," she huffs. "I'll call you later."

I tap the 'off' button and fall back on my little sofa. My sister has been trying to marry me off since before she got married. Why she worries so much is beyond me. In some ways, it's sincere, thoughtful, and protective. In other ways, it's pushy and annoying. She means well, and I believe she would love to be an aunt and watch our family grow. I have been unlucky in the love department up till now. I do have walls up; I can't help it. Sebastian is trying to knock them down, or at least open a doorway in.

I get up off the sofa and step over to my computer, deciding to get lost in my work. Checking through social

173

media and my email, I send a message to my publisher, explaining I have a new book:

I will send you what I have been working on to give you a taste of the material.

I sit back for a second, thinking she will be thrilled to receive these pages. About two minutes later, I receive a reply from Ramona Lacy Publishing:

Thank God, Sharie. I can't wait to read what you have. Would love to see a few more, too...when will this be ready for edit?

Hugs,

Ramona

I laugh out loud, shaking my head. I have really got some pushy broads in my life, between my sister, my publisher, and even Prudence pushing through from the other side. I think, *Maybe I'm just lucky.*

***

I work all day and into the early evening, writing, going through my notes, and working with Prudence's story when my cell phone alerts me back to reality. A text from Bash. I smile as I read the message.

Hello, luv, I miss you. I'm almost done. What are you doing?

I think for a moment then reply:

Just finishing up, too...how about dinner at Rendezvous? Bring your mother, I'm thinking family meeting. ☺

And, Bash quickly responds:

I'll pick you up at 7pm. Love you.

I send him back an

I love you too, see you then.

I check the clock—five-thirty. Just enough time for a shower and change.

In my room, I toss clothes around, wondering what the hell to wear. I want to look good for Bash. It dawns on me how much I care and how I subconsciously included him and his mother in a family meeting. My head spins a little and I sit on the bed.

My sister's bones may be right. I love Bash. No denying it. Could he be the one? My stomach flutters and feels achy but in a good way. My palms start to sweat and my heart beats loud. I realize this feels a little different. I'm a little older, wiser. So is Bash.

I quickly go through the pros: We fit together. He's hot. Sex is mind-blowing. He instantly bonded with my family. Thoughts of my parents rush in. I know they would have loved him; everything about him is sincere, true. He is gentle.

Now cons: He travels a lot for work. Honestly, for me, that could be filed under the pros. On one hand I could easily travel with him, and on the other, I do love to be alone when I'm working on a book. Shit! I couldn't think of one con…It's still early in the relationship, though. Maybe after a while I'll find something. Nobody's perfect; neither am I.

My mind wanders in and out. Thoughts of my life with Bash come into focus as I shower and dress. I decide to stop over-thinking and stick to my plan. Let up off the brakes, let him in just enough. Have fun. I consider myself lucky or blessed. A fantastic guy loves me. I finally get a point.

***

Bash is right on time, and we get to my sister's restaurant a few minutes later. Cornelia is happy and very much looking forward to dinner. We enter, and Jaqueline is the first to see us. "Auntie Shree!" she yells across the dining room. I give a quick glance around. Not that many people, but the bar is still noisy enough to rival her volume level. I wave as she runs in our direction.

Before she can reach me, Bash intercepts and picks her up. "Hello, little lady. You have a hug for me?" he asks. Hearty giggles roll out of Jaqueline as she hugs him around the neck. He places her into a seat, helps me with mine, then takes the chair between us, stating he is in the middle of his two favorite girls besides his mum.

Jaqueline corrects him: "MOM," she says firmly.

Raising his hand, Bash surrenders. "Oh sorry—*mom*. Better?" He winks at her. She purses her lips and nods. We all laugh. I take Bash's hand and give him a reassuring squeeze. He leans in and brushes his lips lightly to mine.

Charlotte comes out of the kitchen to say hello and tell us the specials before the waiter can, then she sends over a wonderful bottle of wine with Jack. We order, and once again my sister doesn't disappoint. She comes out of the kitchen with a plate for herself and eats with us, taking advantage of it being a slow night of the week for the restaurant.

After dinner, we start to discuss our little situation. The topic of conversation gets serious, and Charlotte tells the kids to go play with their video games at another table.

Jack raises his hands. "Listen, I have an idea."

CHAPTER EIGHTEEN

My brother–in-law directs his attention right to me. "Sharie, let me call Ford. He may be able to help with this and keep it private.

I lean my head to the side, a little confused. "Who's Ford?" I ask.

Jack rolls his eyes at me. "Ford Paxton…they remodeled your first floor, made your office. He, Bobby Norrland, and the guys—they were working on your house for almost two months."

"OH! Right," I say, remembering. I look over to Bash. "These guys are the ones who tore down the wall and found the voodoo stuff. They were not thrilled about that, Jack." I glance back to him. "It kind of scared them."

"Huh? Really?" he questions. "They don't seem the type to scare easy."

"Jack," Bash asks, "why do you want to call these particular men? Do you know them well? Can they keep this clandestine?"

Jack's eyes move from Bash to me, then to my sister, who nods her head once. "Yes, I believe so. I have known Ford since high school," Jack says with a reassuring smile. "I can just ask him what he thinks. He may know someone better for this job. I know he won't say anything unless he knows he can trust them, as well."

I toss Bash a glance. "Well, it's worth a shot. Or else I'm the one going out there with a shovel." Cornelia winces at my suggestion.

My sister, sipping carefully at her latte, puts a finger in the air. "I have a question: How do you get her remains to England? You can't just go on a plane and go through security with them."

Bash and his mother look at each other for a second as if they are reading each other's mind. "The yacht," Bash says. "We'll sail back to England on my yacht. I'll let the crew know to prepare for a departure coming up soon."

Charlotte and Jack speak in unison. "You have a yacht?!"

I chuckle. "Yes, he does. I've seen it. It's beautiful." I turn to Bash. "That a great idea...I wasn't even thinking that far ahead."

Cornelia, still sipping on her wine and savoring it, raises her glass. "It's a lovely time of year to sail. Brilliant. I can't wait."

Bash's face collapses as he hears his mother's excitement. "Mother, I'm sorry, but...I was going to send you home on a plane...ahead of us. The journey may be too long for you to go on."

I squeeze his arm, feeling bad for Cornelia as she gulps up her last sip of wine.

"I was not born yesterday, Sebastian. If you want to sail alone with Sharie, just say so. But, I could handle the journey just fine."

"Bash." I give him a look before turning to his mother. "I would love if you came, Cornelia. The yacht is what...like 80 feet long? There is plenty of room for all of us. I'm sure he wasn't suggesting that at all," I assure her while still glaring at him.

He raises an eyebrow at me, his look cunning. "Yes, of course there is room. And, it's a 120-footer. Mum's right, you know. I want you all to myself."

I gasp and look back at Cornelia. She smiles and winks at me. I tap Bash's arm. "You're terrible!" Both he and his mother laugh.

"Okay, fine...Mother, you know you are welcome to join us." He glances over to Jack. "Are you all coming as well?"

Charlotte's eyes go wide "Oh, no...we don't need to go. Do we?" She looks at Jack, who seems to be pondering the idea.

"We could use a little vacation, but sailing to England would take too long for us, and the kids have school."

"It's almost Easter. Don't the kids have spring break around that time, too?" I suggest.

My sister nods her head. "Yes, so flying would be better and quicker for us."

I turn back to Bash. "How long is it going to take us to get there on the yacht?"

He inhales sharply, putting his hand to his chin for a scratch. "I believe it may take ten to twelve days, maybe longer, and that's if we have smooth water and good weather the whole time. We have a small crew, and they'll know what supplies are needed to prepare for the trip."

Cornelia lightly claps her delicate hands in celebration. "It's all settled, then. As soon as we know when we can retrieve Prudence, we will make arrangements. You will all stay at Devonshire House."

At that, we lift our glasses and coffee mugs and make a toast. A plan is in motion. Jack will make a phone call tomorrow to his friend, and hopefully we can end this nightmare and take Prudence home. Once reunited with her family, she should finally be at rest and we will be at peace.

***

A whole day has passed when Jack finally calls me.

"Sharie, I talked with Ford. He and Bobby are going to handle this. They will stop by tomorrow. Show them where the site is. Ford understood our desire for secrecy and didn't ask questions. So, he doesn't know much. Just that we need an area dug and we can handle the rest."

"Great. I can only imagine what he must be thinking, Jack."

"Don't worry about it. They do stuff like this all the time, and it's tax-free money. Ford said to pay him cash. He'll let us know how much after the job is done, since we haven't a clue how deep to dig."

I run my fingers through my hair, massaging my scalp and neck. I'm feeling tense. "I can't imagine it's going to be very deep," I surmise. "Thanks, Jack. I'll call you later."

The next day, Ford and Bobby ring my doorbell. Making small talk at first, I quickly change the subject and ask them if they would like to see the area in question. Ford grabs some wooden stakes and yellow tape from his truck. They follow me out to the path. It's a bright, blue-sky day as we hike toward the big oak tree. When we're finally near, I show them right where I need them to dig.

Ford pulls out the stakes and walks the area, embedding them into the dirt around the plant-like bush I now know is belladonna. An image of Brandy flashes through my mind, and for an instant I'm far away in thought, remembering what she did the other night and what happened to Prudence so long ago.

"You all right, Miss Donovan?" Bobby asks.

"Huh?" His question trips me back into focus. "What did you say, Bobby?"

He stares at me oddly. "I asked if you were all right...hey, where did you just go?"

Now I return his look and let out a little chuckle. "You...uhh...saw that, huh? It's nothing. I'm working on a book, and I can get lost in my thoughts, sometimes. That's all."

"Bobby!" Ford yells at him. "Come over here and help me with the tape. Leave Miss Donovan alone."

Bobby struts over to help Ford. I glance at him, and he nods his head at me, once, as if to tell me not to worry, they won't get nosey.

When they finish surrounding the area with the tape, Ford walks a few steps towards me, takes off his ball cap, and wipes at the perspiration on his forehead with a handkerchief. "That should do it for today. Now, me and Bobby, here, are gonna get this done for you, but I can't get to it till the first of the week. Just finishing a job at the fish camp, up at old Creek Inn on the Bayou. We will get out here early Monday. Is the crack of dawn all right with you?"

I wrinkle my nose. "Monday, huh? Can't do it sooner?"

Ford glances back at Bobby then to me. "Look," he says, lowering his voice, "I don't know what the whole story is, and truth be told, I don't want to know. But Jack told me enough to know that whatever is buried under there has been there a long-assed time. So I figure six more days won't make a difference."

I feel my stomach turn and my eyes grow wide.

"Now," he continues, "don't you worry about a thing. No one knows nothin'—not even Bobby. Just me, and I only know what I need to know. Don't be surprised if I should come alone on Monday. Still trying to figure whose mouth is the least big." He glances back at Bobby.

I smile. "Thanks, Ford. I appreciate that."

He puts his ball cap back on his head and gives me a nod. "Just glad I can help. Jack and I go a long ways back. He's good people. We always help each other." Ford looks around, then, at Bobby, who appears to be lost in his own world and texting on his cell phone. "Hey, let's go, Bobby. We're still on the clock."

"What are ya talkin' about? You're the boss," Bobby says smiling childishly.

"Yep, I am, and you're on my clock. Now, move your ass."

Ford and Bobby follow me home, then get in the truck and drive off. I sit on my front porch, feeling like a mixed bowl of nuts. I really thought they would have dug today or tomorrow. I feel down, but thrilled; worried, but relieved. Just then, I am pleasantly surprised to see Bash pull up. I stand as he comes to me up the sidewalk. I peek at my phone. "Shouldn't you be working?" I joke. "It's not five o'clock, yet."

He stops short. "Sorry. You want me to leave?"

I give him a long stare as if to think about it. "Never," I answer.

He saunters slowly to me and wraps me in his arms, kisses me hard, and dips me back. With his strong hands, I am in a secure grip. His mouth pulls away suddenly, and he nips my bottom lip. Once. Twice. And, with his cute little smirk says, "Honey, I'm home."

***

Over an order of Chinese takeout, he and I talk about the plan Ford had explained to me just before Bash arrived.

"I wanted to be here today with you when they came. I'm sorry I missed them by a few minutes."

I pick up a carton of dumplings. Carefully spearing one with a chopstick, I bite it in half. "You really didn't miss much," I say. "They staked out the area and…that was that. Said they'd be back on Monday. Seemed odd the way Ford was being all secretive, even in front of Bobby." I shrug. "Like I told you, I'm not happy about it. I wanted it done as soon as possible, but it is what it is, I guess."

Bash swaps his Kung Pao with my dumplings. "So, they are finishing a job elsewhere and they can't get to it until Monday. Well, I can see that. But, Ford being suspicious of Bobby does seem rather peculiar."

"That's what I thought. He also wanted to make sure who he could trust. Maybe Bobby has a big mouth," I suggest. "Ford said he might come back by himself."

Bash wipes his mouth and takes a pull from his beer. "I hope he figures that out. The fewer we have who know, the better. It would be more logical for him to do it alone. What is going to happen when they find…it?"

"Prudence," I say with a hint of sarcasm. "Well, I was hoping to be there along with Brandy and maybe…your mother?"

"Really? Why?" he asks, going after the fried rice, next.

"Because, the three of us have a connection to Prudence. And, I know Brandy will want to do some kind of prayer. I thought maybe Jaqueline, too, but she's so young and I have no idea what we'll find. Having her at the reburial will be enough."

His face gets serious, with his chin jutting out and a small wrinkle creasing his brow. "I want to be here for you, too, Sharie, but I'm leaving for New York tomorrow afternoon and I'll be back sometime on Saturday or Sunday. So, I'm pleased that I will be here with you on Monday." His expression changes and he puts on his smirk that I love.

"My mother will be at the condo, and I know she would really like to see you again. She, uh, told me she's fond of you and thinks very highly of you."

I raise my eyes from my food. Bash's eyebrows are raised and he has a closed-lip smile.

"I don't know what to say. I mean, I figured she likes me, but that was very sweet of her to say."

"Who could not love you, Sharie? I told my mother the first time I met you I was fond of you from the start. You have that kind of personality. You, my love, make me extremely happy."

After dinner, we snuggle on the sofa and watch a movie. Soon after, we're in bed making love. Bash tells me I am almost too much for him to handle. *Funny*, I think, *I feel the same about him.* His stamina seems higher or stronger than that of any man I've ever known. I am very aware of my own body's craving for him. Just to look at him, I get excited and heat floods my core. Again I wonder, *Is this true love?* I roll over and gaze at Bash while he sleeps, and my stomach swirls. My breath catches and I know. Now I know.

Bash stays with me and works from the house in my office until he leaves for the airport. I decide to call Brandy to let her know of the upcoming plans.

"I will absolutely be there," she says. "Starting this weekend is a dark moon, so really, it's perfect."

"I'm not sure I'm making that connection, Brandy."

I hear her laugh lightly. "A dark moon, Sharie, indicates a time for release. That could be taken many ways. A clearing out or getting rid of stuff, especially bad energy. A time to get ready for renewed energy to be reborn."

"That sounds good to me. Kind of goes along with the fact we are in the Lenten season with Easter being two weeks away."

"Yes, Sharie. That's also a time for reflection and renewal. Other types of powers come into play around this time, too. But remember—always with good there might be bad. A predator lurking. Light the sage I gave you for protection, and wear Lisette's pendant."

I smile though she can't see me. "I will, Brandy. See you soon."

CHAPTER NINETEEN

Early that afternoon, I drive over to Sebastian's penthouse.

I had asked Cornelia in the morning if she wanted to have lunch. She was thrilled and said she would be ready by noon. Leaving my car behind, we use one of Bash's Mercedes with his personal driver to take us out for the day. We head up the coast about an hour towards Biloxi and decide that lunching at the Beau Rivage hotel and casino would be a fun afternoon.

"This is lovely here, dear. Thank you for inviting me out."

I smile and touch her arm. "No problem. With Bash away for a few days, no reason for you to stay alone. I'm happy you wanted to come."

Cornelia closes her eyes as a smile spreads across her tiny, pink mouth. "I truly am so glad we are spending some time alone, Sharie. I must confess, at first I didn't know what your intensions toward my son were. First, I learned you had purchased Ravensdale Manor. Then, Sebastian told me about what was behind the wall. Well, you can understand I was frightened—frightened of what was found and that you or the house might harm my son."

She put her hands to her face as if to wipe away a bad memory. "Sharie, I am so relieved you have stayed and didn't get scared off. All those years, the stories that surrounded generations, now we know the truth." She shivers and shakes her head, a serious expression appearing in those icy-blue eyes.

"You know what I'd like to do, Sharie? Document what we have found out. You know—write it down. Maybe create some kind of family-tree book like Brandy and Ophelia have. I strongly feel I must do this. It is, after all, part of the Ravensdale/Devonshire history. And it's all because of you." She taps my hand. "You are so brave. Very brave indeed."

"Thank you, Cornelia. I think it's a great idea. I can help you. Maybe you could look at my notes for your documentation. Now, as for me being brave?" I shrug a shoulder. "I didn't know what was happening to me, but then…I never felt like I was in any danger. It was a relief when Jaqueline told me she saw Prudence and was not afraid. I think knowing that helped me a lot. I also believe Prudence did her best not to frighten us. She just told her sad story through me and somehow conveyed her feelings to me along with it. I knew it was more distress than anything else. We are close, I think, to Prudence having closure and being at peace." I sit back in my chair with a fresh, hot latte while Cornelia sips her tea.

"You have been very open and receptive to all this, dear. That's why I think you're so brave."

I place my latte on the table. "You know, both my parents are gone now, yet with all that has happened I feel hopeful. I had lost my faith and hope in many ways, but I am relieved to know this isn't all there is, the end." I swipe my hands. "Maybe your husband, my parents, and all other loved ones are not really gone, just waiting somewhere for us...whether it's heaven or another dimension. I have a new-found perspective; it's what I needed. I didn't believe I would ever find love again—I'd lost faith in that, too—until Bash. I'm still a little nervous about it."

Cornelia stares into space for a minute, then she smiles warmly. "Don't you worry about Sebastian. He is absolutely smitten with you. I've never seen the sparkle so bright in his eyes, never seen him attach himself to a woman so completely before. And, never has he told me he has loved any other before you."

My head snaps up. "He's told you he loves me?"

"Oh yes, dear, quite a few times. So, don't you worry about him. I have no doubt of the love he has for you, Sharie." She hesitates for just a second then leans closer to me. "I also am very fond of you, dear. My son has good taste." She winks.

For the rest of the afternoon, we shop at some stores and gamble in the casino. I play a few slot machines and find out Cornelia really likes blackjack. She is on a winning streak and getting very rambunctious with the dealer and the other players. It's very tempting to sit down and play, but I choose to hang back, to laugh along with her and the other gamblers.

By the time we arrive back at Sebastian's penthouse, the sun is setting. I hug her goodbye. "Well, I guess I'll see you on Monday during the dig?"

"Yes, my dear, I will be there. I told Sebastian I will call the captain tomorrow and tell him to get the yacht ready. He and the crew will have a lot of work to do to get the *Dark Horse* ready to sail across the Atlantic."

"Yes, it's going to be a long trip," I add, stating the obvious.

"It'll be fun and relaxing as long as you have good weather. Don't tell Sebastian, but I've been thinking he is right. I might not be able to handle two weeks on the water. I may fly home ahead of you and wait for everyone at Devonshire House. You're going to love it there, Sharie."

"I'm sure I will," I say as I hug her goodbye one more time. "Sleep well. I'll talk to you soon." I turn and get in my car to leave while thoughts of sailing pop into my head.

My cell phone rings, bringing me back to land. "Hi, Bash," I answer.

"Hello, luv. Where are you?"

"I just left your mom at your place. I had a wonderful day. I learned many things. True fact, your mother loves to play blackjack!"

"Oh God, did she get out of control? It can be quite an embarrassing scene," he laughs.

"Not at all. She had fun, we had fun. Oh, I just found out the name of your yacht is the *Dark Horse*! I get it—because of the horse problem in the polo match, right?"

"Very perceptive you are, Ms. Donovan. I am glad you went out with Mother, today. I am missing you tremendously already. I love you, Sharie. Sleep well, darling."

"Love you, too, Bash. Get home soon and safe."

***

Late the next morning, my doorbell rings. I stop working to go answer it.

"Morning, Miss Donovan. Hope I didn't disturb you."

It's Bobby. At first I'm confused, but then I get my hopes up thinking he's here to get started on the digging. "No worries, Bobby. You guys going to dig?"

"No, Ma'am. That's what I'm here to tell you. We ran into a problem, and it might be a week before we can come out to do the work for you."

Like a deflated balloon, my hopes sink to the floor. "Are you joking? What kind of problem, Bobby?"

"The job at the fish camp had a little problem. There was a gas leak, so we might not be done by Monday. I just wanted to come by and notify you."

"I am not pleased about this, Bobby. I need to get this situation taken care of as soon as possible."

Bobby cocks his head to the side, squinting at me in the late-morning sun. "What kind of situation you got? Why do you want a hole dug out there next to the big oak? You got somethin' to bury or to get out?"

I stand quietly for a minute. My eyesight narrows on him as I ponder his question. "No, Bobby I just need to get something done. I'm sorry. I can't discuss it with you. Thanks for dropping by, but I might need to call someone

192

else. Please tell Ford thanks for his time, but his schedule is clearly too busy to help me."

"Will do, Miss Donovan. You have a nice a day."

He walks from my front porch and back to his truck. I slam the door shut. Furious, I stomp all over the house like a child. I know there is only one thing left to do: dig and find Prudence myself.

Out in my shed, I find two different-sized shovels. I truly don't know how I am going to dig enough by myself, but pure adrenalin, fueled by frustration, is driving me crazy by now.

I pause for a moment to consider Bash, but I figure it will be done by the time he gets back home. I call Brandy to tell her what I'm about to do because of new circumstance. She advises me to wait until tomorrow since she will be available all afternoon and is eager to help me.

I take the shovels and bring them inside, placing them by the back door, ready for tomorrow. Nothing else to do except wait. I feel jittery and out of place not knowing what to do with myself in the meantime. No Bash, and it's Friday night, so my sister is working. I will call her first thing in the morning to tell her plans have changed.

***

Walking in the dark woods, the wet grass on my bare feet, a foggy mist surrounds me...I have been here in this place and time before. Somehow, I know what's coming—Prudence in the nun's habit. I squint because I remember her skeletal face, her claw-like hand holding her locket. It scares me. I see her, a dark, shadowy image hiding under a veil. She is pointing to where she is buried. "Prudence," I say calmly, "we're coming to get you tomorrow and take you to be with your family." She turns slightly and walks over her grave and disappears. I run to her. "Prudence!" I shout, "Prudence, where are you?" I circle the area, but I trip over the tape that outlines where to dig. I fall, the ground opens, and I'm plummeting. I feel weightless...

I sit up and take in a big breath. I'm home in my bed. Just the first shreds of daylight seep in between the slats of the shutters on my windows. *Just another dream.* I wipe the perspiration from my forehead. "Okay, Prudence," I say aloud, "today is the day."

I get up, make strong coffee, and call my sister. I tell her there is a new plan in place.

"Oh for Christ's sake, Sharie. You can't go digging up the ground. Wait for us; Jack will help. I can't believe Bobby told you they can't do it until next week, because Ford spoke to Jack yesterday and said you cancelled the dig!"

"What time was that, Charlotte? Bobby was here around eleven a.m. and told me they ran into a problem at another job. I told him how displeased I was and that I would have to call someone else. But, I don't care, Char. I need to move forward on this. If you and Jack want to help me, great! Brandy will be here by three p.m. I'm hoping I have a good-sized hole dug by then."

"Sharie, just wait for us to get there. I can stay until Brandy shows up, but then I have to go to work. Jack and the kids will stay with you. Dear God, I hope you know what you're doing."

"I think I do," I say very reassuringly. "I actually feel better knowing I'm doing it than having someone come out here. I think it's better…I think Prudence agrees, too. Yep, feeling good about it. Can't explain it, but I do."

"When is Bash getting home?" Charlotte asks.

"Later tonight or first thing in the morning. I haven't really heard from him. Just a text here and there."

I hear her sigh. "And, you don't want to wait for him? The guys can help you better than I can."

My fingers squeeze the phone as I pace the floors. "Charlotte, shut up! I love you, but please, I'm not helpless…I don't need a man to dig a hole. Yes, their help would make it go faster, but I'm not helpless, and I'm too jittery to sit still."

"Okay, okay…Shit! I'm just afraid of you going out there by yourself. We are dealing with a supernatural force. We don't know what can happen."

I stop in my tracks. She's got a point. *Shit!*

"Okay, Char, you might be right. I have some things that may help before I go out there. The protection pendant and some sage. Brandy told me to use these before anyone was going to dig. She also told me there is a dark moon rising this weekend, which helps in some ways but can also allow other kinds of predators in."

"What do you mean *predators*? I don't like the sound of that."

"I think she meant other predatory spirits—I hope."

"Be careful, Sharie. We will see you in a few hours."

"Okay. I'll be out by the big oak."

After disconnecting the call, I run upstairs, pull my hair back into a ponytail, and slip on some old, worn-out jeans with holes in the knees and an old blue T-shirt of Dad's. It's a size or so too big but perfect for the job today.

I couldn't part with some of the things that had belonged to my parents. Why I specifically kept this old rag of a shirt with the sleeves cut off, I don't know. I have a fond memory of Dad mowing the lawn in it, and for some reason wearing it felt like more protection. I stuff my feet into my sneakers and dart back downstairs.

I make one more phone call to Cornelia, but she doesn't answer, so I leave a message. Placing my cell phone on the kitchen counter, I use both hands to slip the pendant over my head. Then, picking up the sage, I light it the way Brandy told me to. I walk through the house with the burning ember, which smells sweet and peppery. I say the prayer:

"Bless this home with your pure, white light of love and protection. Banish all negative energies from this house with the energy of love and light.

"Smoke and air, fire and earth, cleanse and bless this home and hearth. Drive away all harm and fear. Only good may enter here."

I repeat it over and over while walking through each room, door, and closet. Then, over my computer. I decide to burn the sage all the way to the oak tree and around Prudence's grave. I pick up the two shovels and go out the back door, leaving it unlocked for my sister.

I get to the path with the burning herb, repeating the prayers a few more times as I go.

CHAPTER TWENTY

Cornelia shuffles out of her steam-filled bathroom and enters the dining room to sit down and eat a breakfast fit for a queen. The housekeeper places today's paper and her cell phone next to her.

"Thank you, dear." Eyeing the blinking blue light indicating a voice message, she promptly checks and sees it's Sharie.

"Hi, Cornelia. Plans have changed. Long story. I am digging Prudence up myself, today. I would love it very much if you could be here. Talk soon."

"She's going to dig? By herself? Today! What on earth?" She dials Sharie's phone, but it goes straight to voice mail. Then, she dials Sebastian.

"Hello, Mother. How are you?"

"Sebastian, where are you?"

"Believe it or not, in flight. I took off about an hour ago. Is everything all right?"

"I don't know, son. The other day, I had a wonderful afternoon with Sharie. She told me they were digging Monday. But I just received a voice message that plans have changed. She's going out there to do it herself. She asked me to go over. I wanted to tell you that's where we'll be, today. I haven't a clue about what went wrong with the original plan. I tried to call, but she's not answering."

"I see. Thanks for the heads up. I'm going to make a few calls. Did you call Captain Pete?"

"Yes, the yacht will be ready for Tuesday morning."

"Call him back, Mother. Tell him I'm sorry for the inconvenience, but plans have changed. We may have to go out earlier than we'd anticipated."

Sebastian hangs up with his mother and calls Sharie, but there still is no answer. Thinking for a moment, he dials Jack.

"Hey, Bash, you back in town?"

"Not yet, Jack. I'm in the air on my way. I can't reach Sharie. What is going on? What has changed?"

"Yeah, it's weird, Bash. Sharie told us that Bobby went over to the house, said they can't dig until next week because of a problem at another job. So, I call my buddy Ford and ask him what the deal is. He hasn't got a clue. He says Sharie saw Bobby out at the store, told him she found someone else for the job. Ford has been trying to call Bobby all morning but can't find him. Sharie, being stubborn, went out there on her own to start digging. We're on our way there, now."

Sebastian runs a hand through his brown locks. "Okay, good. I'm glad you're going over there. I'm not happy about what I'm hearing, Jack. What do you know about this Bobby?"

"Quiet dude. Has a girlfriend. Not real bright, if you catch my drift, but nice enough guy. Big in their church. Never had a record, if that's what you mean."

198

"I don't know…but thanks, Jack. I'll be landing shortly. I'll be there as soon as I can."

A million things run through Sebastian's mind. He had the feeling something like this would happen. He also suspected Sharie would go for it on her own. Jack knew her well—stubborn. But, *determined* is what Sebastian would call it. The thought of her digging in the middle of the woods, alone, crosses his mind and he thinks maybe she's a little pig-headed, too. But, after all, that is one of many things he adores about her. Her strong will for something she wants. Yes, he supposes some may see Sharie as stubborn, but he sees her as bold and valiant.

***

I drop the shovels as I get to the big oak. I continue with the sage, repeating the prayers while walking around Prudence's grave. When I feel the area is good and clean, I snuff out the sage and pick up one of the shovels. I go to check the time but realize I've left my phone on the kitchen counter. *Shit!* I figure Jack will be smart enough to bring it to me when he gets here.

I slowly remove the tape along with some of the stakes. Pushing the shovel into the ground with all my might and the help of my foot, I'm able lift a nice little piece of sod and toss it aside.

After what seems like an hour, sweat begins to form across my forehead and drip down the back of my neck. I should have brought gloves. My palms are getting raw, even though it seems I've only just begun. Hence, help would have been a good idea, I grudgingly admit to myself.

I wonder where everyone is. I take a little break before I shovel a few more piles.

I hear the woods crackle and I think, *Thank God Jack made it!* I turn and say, "Hey, just in time—" but it's Bobby standing there gazing at me as I stop cold, shovel in hand, knee-deep in dirt.

"Bobby? What are you doing here?"

"Miss Donovan, looks like we're gonna have a bit of a problem. Seems to me you're digging up something that should stay dead and buried."

I am quiet for a moment, confused about what is happening. I choose my words very carefully. "Oh? What makes you say that, Bobby?"

"I'm not so dumb, Miss Donovan. I know what you're doin'—and it ain't right. Witches need to stay buried. Only reason why someone would want to dig up a witch is if she is a witch, herself."

"Whoa…Now wait a minute, Bobby. I'm not a witch and neither was Prudence. She dabbled in some voodoo, but it's not witchcraft. Where did you hear such lies? Who told you about this?"

"I grew up around these parts. Some of us know the story of the witch in Ravensdale Manor. I know why you wanted that wall knocked out. You wanted the voodoo stuff. You knew it was there. I didn't believe it till I saw it with my own eyes. That witch got what she deserved. Me and the girlfriend, Darla, we go to the Fist of Fury church. We know how to repel all that is evil and unclean. I didn't want to believe a nice woman like yourself could be dark, so I been watchin'. Then, today, I smelled that witch fire you was burnin'…and I knew what you was gonna do."

I stand motionless, astonished by his words. I thought maybe this was a joke of some kind. "Witch fire? No, Bobby that's white sage. It cleanses the area of anything evil. You have it all wrong. You've been brainwashed by that crazy church!"

He looks at me with lunacy in his eyes as he corrects the name as though it's a prayer. "FIST. OF. FURY. We are pure and holy."

I wrinkle my nose. "Sounds more like the church of the dazed and confused. They don't make you drink fruit punch that tastes funny, do they?"

"You pokin' fun at us, Miss Donovan? Why, this just tells me you're too far gone. I'm gonna have to ask you to drop that shovel and come with me."

I eye him up and down. "Yeah…I don't think so, Bobby. I have a job to do here. I have to make right what went horribly wrong a long time ago. An innocent woman was murdered, but it wasn't really about witchcraft. That was a big lie started by a very bad man to turn the town against her. Now, please leave. Oh—and, Bobby, get some help. Stay away from that church."

"I thought that's how it might go down with you, a woman on her own practicing witchcraft. I didn't wanna do this, but you give me no choice…"

I freeze in my spot. This dude has lost his mind. I go for my pocket but remember there's no cell phone in it. If I yell, no one will hear me. But, if they are close, they will come running. I decide to stay quiet. I don't want to freak Bobby out and make any sudden movements, because this asshole just might use the gun that's now pointed at my head.

Jack, Charlotte, and the kids pull up to Sharie's house and scurry around to the back door to let themselves in.

Charlotte eyes Sharie's cell sitting there on the counter. "Aha! Now I know why we couldn't reach her. She must have forgotten it."

"Mom, what's with the funky smell?" Charlie cries out.

Charlotte sniffs the air. "Sage? Yes, I believe it's sage. Aunt Sharie must be burning it."

"Eww…why?"

"Its cleansing, or for protection. Your nose will get used to it."

Jack puts down a few grocery bags and looks around. "I guess she's already out there. I'll go out now and take her phone to her, too. She has a ton of missed calls."

"Oh—wait!" Charlotte calls out, putting up her hands. "Take some water bottles. Knowing my sister, she didn't take any along, and she's probably thirsty."

Jack follows his wife to the fridge and grabs a few beers, instead. Charlotte rolls her eyes at him. "What?" he shrugs. "Knowing your sister, she's gonna want beer first, then water."

"Momma! Momma, come here!" Jaqueline's tiny voice pinches through the air like a siren. They all sprint to the office. Jaqueline's eyes are wide, watching Friedo barking and scratching at the door like crazy.

"What's wrong, sweetie? You're scaring me!"

Jaqueline points at the door. "The lady is very upset. She is so sad, Momma. She wants us to go out!"

Charlotte takes hold of Jaqueline's arms. "What is it? Tell me what you see!"

"The lady." Jaqueline puts her hands to her ears. "The buzzing! Make it stop, Momma."

"Jaqueline, baby, calm down. Try to tell me what she's showing you!"

"I can't…I can't. It's too loud. The lady is…the lady is…" Jaqueline's eyes shut and she goes stiff in her mother's hands.

"No—don't hurt her, Prudence! My baby!"

Jack and Charlie come close. Jaqueline's eyes open, and the cornflower-blue color is milky. Her movements are stiff, robot-like. *"Sharie…danger…chene…"*

In a flash, it is over. Jaqueline is back and doesn't even know what had happened. "Momma, is Auntie Shree hurt?"

Charlotte gazes at her daughter and hugs her close. "Oh God, Jack! Prudence is warning us! Sharie must be in some kind of danger."

"I'm on it! Does Sharie have a gun, Char?"

"Yes, Daddy's shotgun, upstairs in her bedroom."

***

"Please don't shoot me, Bobby. I'm not a bad person. You're confused. You don't know the whole story; I do. I researched everything, even talked to people who know the truth about how she ended up here and why she was beaten and hung. I'm going write a book about it, all of it."

"A book about a witch written by a witch. Now step out of that hole, drop the shovel, and sit over by the tree. Don't pull anything tricky. I will shoot you."

I drop the shovel and walk the few steps over to the big oak tree. I notice a shiny handle sticking out of tall grass and leaves. The other shovel, laying there right where I'd left it.

***

Jack grabs the shotgun and checks to see if it's loaded. It is. He puts his cell phone in his pocket and looks at his wife. "Stay here. Lock yourselves in. Call the restaurant, and tell them they are on their own tonight—we may have a family emergency."

"Be careful, Jack. You don't know what you're walking into!"

"I'll sneak in, just in case. I'll text you if I need you to call the cops. If she's there alone and hurt, I'll call an ambulance then tell you. Got it?" He gives her a quick kiss and heads out the back door.

Sharie's cell phone chimes, and Charlotte grabs it quickly when she sees it's Bash. "Bash! It's Charlotte. Something has happened! Sharie is in some kind of danger!"

"I'm on the ground and getting an air lift to my building. I should be there soon. What's happened?"

Charlotte explains the horrific scene as the doorbell rings; it's Brandy. Charlotte lets her in and recaps the same story of what has transpired in the last twenty minutes.

Brandy takes a few steps over to Jaqueline. "Hi, baby, how are you doing? Do you feel okay?" Jaqueline nods her head and gives her a big smile. "You are a brave little girl, just like your auntie." Brandy looks at Charlotte, who is now staring out the window and holding two cell phones. "Why don't you go and give your momma some of that bravery. She looks like she could use some."

Brandy watches as Jaqueline bops on her tiptoes to her mother and the two hug tightly. Brandy picks up her big satchel and opens the back door. "I'm going out there. Don't worry—I'll stay hidden."

"You can't go out there! You might get hurt. My husband's out there with a gun and God only knows what else!"

"Charlotte, please stay calm. It's going to be fine. I will be fine."

CHAPTER TWENTY-ONE

I glare at Bobby, who is still pointing the gun at me. I have a million emotions stirring in my veins. The biggest one—anger. I am angry that this idiot has been brainwashed, that he is holding me at gun point. I'm furious that he might take me or someone else out because of closed-minded stupidity. I try to breathe and to reason with him.

"Hey, Bobby. You're not really going to use that, are you? Why don't we talk about what is going on here? I can explain it to you."

"No thanks, witch. You're not gonna try to poison me with your lies. Stay outta my head. What you're doin' here is just plain immoral. It's blasphemy!"

I lower my head. I feel my patience tapering off. "Bobby, I'm not a witch...I-I'm a writer. I write about mystery and romance. I'm no witch! The stories that have been told to you are lies."

"Shut up! I'm callin' my pastor. He's gonna tell me what to do with you next."

I put my hands to my forehead. "Oh, great..."

Then, just as he is reaching for his cell, I hear what sounds like the snap of twigs. Bobby turns frantically around and shoots the gun straight up in the air.

"I have a gun here!" he yells. "I'll shoot her and you!" He turns back in my direction. His eyes appear crazier. "Looks like we're gonna have a party."

The next sound I hear is a rock cracking into a tree just a few feet away from Bobby. Distracted and stunned, he turns his head quickly toward the sound, while his arm is still pointing the gun toward me. I quickly grab the other shovel and swing it like a bat right into his forearm, with full force. The gun flies from his grip, and I kick it out of the way. He drops to his knees, holding his arm, as I give him another blunt blow to his head.

I drop to the ground, too, feeling as though the wind has been knocked out of my lungs from pure adrenaline.

"Holy shit!" Panting, I look up and see Jack coming towards me with Daddy's shotgun. Then, like a miracle, Bash is sprinting in from behind him.

"Sharie! My God! Are you all right?" Bash demands as he helps me to my feet.

"Yes, I think so. Check Bobby. I might have given him a severe headache."

Jack and Bash look over at him. Jack rolls him over. "You broke his wrist." A moan escapes from Bobby. "Oh, that's a good sign—he's moaning. Means he's not dead," Jack surmises sarcastically.

"You hit him?" Bash asks, looking at me with his big, blue, wide-worried eyes.

"Yeah, with the shovel," I answer, feeling a little woozy. "Jack, good idea throwing the rocks! It distracted him."

"Umm, that wasn't me, Sharie, but I wish I had thought of it. I was going to shoot him in the leg, but I couldn't get a clear shot. The bastard wouldn't stand still long enough."

I look questioningly at Bash.

"Wasn't me. I just got here. I ran from the house and found you. I heard a gunshot and thought something terrible had happened to you. My God, Sharie, are you sure you're fine?" He pulls me into his arms, his heart pounding so hard it scares me.

"Hey...calm down," I whisper. "I'm fine, really."

"I threw the rocks." We hear a voice come from another part of the woods. We turn and see Brandy step out from a bunch of trees.

"Brandy! Thank God," I sigh. "I guess I wasn't all alone out here after all."

Brandy smiles and drops her big bag to the ground. "I was watching and listening. I figured the distraction would help you. And, girl, you did not disappoint. You got a mean swing!" She bent down over Bobby. "He's gonna be in and out for a while. Why don't you guys take his sorry ass to the hospital. Me and Sharie have to get down to business before it gets too dark.

Bash and Jack pick up Bobby and his gun and haul him back to the house. I keep Dad's gun with me. Brandy picks up a shovel and gives me a nod. We start to dig, going in a neat oblong. Soon, my sister, Cornelia, and the kids arrive with water and a couple bottles of beer. "Good choice!" I say as I open the beer. "Thanks!"

"Thank Jack—it was his idea," Charlotte said. "He thought you could use it."

Cornelia approaches with caution over to the good-sized hole we've made. "You ladies find anything yet?"

I chuckle. "Not yet, but you'll know it when we do, because I'll probably scream."

Brandy smiles. "No, you won't. I promise it's not as bad as you think. We should be close, now."

I roll my eyes. "Oh sure, how awful can a bag of bones be?"

About fifteen minutes later, I spot something unusual. "Brandy, stop! Look." I point to an area of our shallow hole where what appear to be drawstrings are sticking out of the soil.

Brandy reaches out to touch them. "Silk," she says. "I think we found her."

We dig a little more until I see the faded, purple bag protruding. Brandy gently pulls while I keep moving the dirt to help her get it loose. When it's finally free, we gently bring the bundle over and place Prudence's remains on the ground.

We're all quiet for a moment. Brandy pulls a vile of pink powder out of her satchel and sprinkles it all around the purple bag. She chants something I don't understand then pulls at the drawstrings to open the bag. Thunder cracks and wind twirls violently around us on what had been a clear, sunny day.

A bolt of pink lightning, or what seemed to be lightning, darts between all of us. I gasp, afraid of getting jolted. Brandy grabs my hand. "It's all right, Sharie. Prudence is here. It's her energy. She is happy."

I hear Jaqueline giggle, and that joyful sound helps me overcome any fear. All at once, the pink storm slows and calms. We are back to normal daylight, again. I glance back at the bag.

"Brandy, look!" I gasp. A skeletal forearm is poking out of the bag. I see a silver necklace with a big, oval-shaped locket dangling from a small, bony hand. "Like in my dream," I whisper. I reach for the locket and open it. A miniature family portrait is sealed within. Prudence, Bernard, and three beautiful girls. Everyone comes closer to peer at the find. Etched on the other side is one word, a word I am not familiar with: *Atropa*.

"What is it, Sharie?" Brandy asks.

I hold up the locket and show it to her. "Atropa?" I ask softly. "What does this mean?"

Brandy laughs and nods her head. "I knew it!" she blurts. "I just didn't know how to be sure. Thank you, Prudence and Lisette!" Brandy shouts to the heavens. "Sharie, atropa is *belladonna*! The secret to her absinthe!"

"Are you joking?" I ask with a smile. "The belladonna was the secret herb? It's been right in front of us for weeks!"

I pass the locket to Cornelia, who is crying. "You okay, Cornelia?"

"Yes…yes, I'm fine. Happy tears, dear. You found the truth. I feel very peaceful. Now, off to give Prudence a proper burial where she belongs."

***

That evening, we sit around my dining room table, having a meal and trying to plan out the next few weeks. Bash and Jack also tell us what had happened at the hospital. They had waited for Bobby to come around. When he did, Bash had explained the consequences he would suffer should he come near me again or blab this story to another living soul. Bash had told him, for one thing, he would find a way to have him committed to a facility for the insane for the rest of his life.

Jack, on the other hand, had used a more common approach: "If I ever see you again. I will rip your eyes out so you can watch yourself die from the palm of my hand." Ford had backed up Jack and fired Bobby on the spot. No one had called the police or filed any charges against him. They simply told everyone he had been in a bar brawl.

During our meal, Brandy also explains how Bobby could have been the evil predator she warned me about. "Evil doesn't always have to come from the other side." She also shows me something she brought with her—a little, antique chest for me to bury Prudence's remains in. It's the size of three shoeboxes. A lovely bronze with white-onyx trim and oak leaves etched into the base. Most of Prudence's body had disintegrated, as we suspected. Brandy puts what is left of her in the chest and seals it up.

Bash, who had been on his phone for what seemed to be a while, finally returns to the table. "Pack your bags, luv. I just got off the phone with Captain Pete. We are leaving at the crack of dawn, tomorrow!"

I raise my eyebrows. "Why so soon, Bash? I thought I'd have more time."

"With all that has happened with Bobby, I don't want to linger. Who knows what he told that church. Speaking of which, I intend to have them checked out. Doing the paperwork alone will keep them busy for a few months."

"It's all settled then," Charlotte says. "We will make our flight arrangements when you are close to reaching Devonshire. Have a great trip! Bon voyage!"

Everyone leaves except Bash. I run around the house like a crazy person, trying to get my things in order. I will be gone for about a month. Two weeks on the ocean, then who knows how long it will take to have Prudence buried. I grab suitcases, check weather forecasts, secure windows and doors. I download my manuscript onto a zip drive so I can bring my laptop. My head is spinning. Bash steps into my line of fire and put his hands on my arms.

"Hey, calm down. Believe me, you won't need much. I had some shopping done for you. It's probably already on the boat. Just bring essentials. The house will be fine, too. I can have someone come here to look after things like I used to when my family owned it. They can take care of it."

"Really? You did? You will? For me?" I stutter.

"Sharie, luv, I would do anything for you. I love you. I was out of my mind this afternoon. I thought you had been hurt or shot. I was a bloody mess thinking how close I came to losing you."

His eyes burn into me, and I feel the heat rise with his gentle kiss. His hands search and caress my body, making me moan. He picks me up and places me on the kitchen counter, leans me back, and unzips my jeans, tugging them down along with my underwear. He drives me crazy with a flurry of kisses over my belly and down my legs while he gently pulls my legs farther apart. I feel the lash of his tongue on my damp flesh, making me writhe. He continues relentlessly as my core is aching, needing to be filled. The orgasm hits hard, making me arch my back. He licks until I am so sensitive I jump at his touch.

Scooping me up, he heads for the bedroom. He places me on the bed while quickly removing his own clothes. Climbing on top of me, he kisses my neck, my breasts. He pushes in, fulfilling my body's desire, moving rhythmically, unstoppingly, until we come together in a strong rush of passion.

Snuggled and warm, we rest in each other's arms. Bash has made love to me so deeply. My stomach quivers to think about it. I search his eyes in the dark.

"How am I supposed to keep my hands off you on the yacht? It's such close quarters."

He laughs. "Who says you have to?" He lifts my chin to kiss my mouth. "I'm looking forward to being alone with you, Sharie. I fully intend to have my hands all over you."

I giggle and kiss him back. He nuzzles me in closer "Get some sleep, luv. We need to be on board before seven a.m."

***

I am completely out-of-my-mind tired, grasping a cup of coffee from the local Dunkin' Donuts in my hands. We have made it to Bash's yacht, the *Dark Horse*, right at seven a.m. Cornelia is standing on board, smiling at us.

"Good morning, darlings. My goodness, Sharie. You look utterly exhausted!"

I raise my styrofoam cup to her. "I'm hoping this helps. It's a double espresso."

"No worries, dear. You will sleep like a baby on the water; it is so very relaxing. Plenty of time to catch up on your sleep."

I enter the vessel on the aft deck. It smells clean and new, almost like that new-car smell. To my right is deck seating. Plush, cushioned chairs with tables are bolted down. Bash opens a door and tells me to enter what is called 'the main salon.' It's a beautiful living space with a big-screen T.V. and large, overstuffed navy-blue sofas with aqua and white accent pillows.

A soft, tan carpet has been laid throughout the space, and I see a fully functioning, well-stocked bar at one end. Following Bash up a few steps, I find the galley fully equipped with high-end appliances and a spacious U-shaped settee just behind the three captains' chairs at the helm station.

Bash continues our tour down another set of steps to a carpeted hallway opening into three staterooms. The master has its own, private bathroom or, as Bash calls it, the *loo*.

"I didn't realize how roomy this yacht—or any yacht, for that matter—can be. It sure doesn't look this big from the outside."

"You like her?" Bash asks.

I nod my head in awe. "Yeah...she's beautiful!"

"Come here, luv. I want to show you something."

Back out to the hallway and up more stairs, we walk along the side deck to a small room with windows that overlook the ocean. It appears to be a cute, little office, complete with a lovely wooden desk and smaller captain's chair on one end with Wi-Fi hook ups. Bookshelves and pictures occupy the interior walls. All this is surrounded by a nautical/pirate décor that is cozy and quaint yet tasteful.

"Very nice. Is this your office?"

He smiles a gleaming white grin that reaches up to his indigo eyes. "No, luv, it's your office."

My eyes grow so wide I think they might pop out. "Wait...What? My office? You don't have to..." He shuts me up with a kiss and continues until he can feel me relax and turn to mush in his hands.

"It's my gift for you. We will be at sea for the greater part of ten to fourteen days, maybe longer. You'll need a place to write where you can be alone—just you, the sea, and your thoughts."

I spin around in place. "I don't know what to say! I don't believe you've done this for me. No one has ever..." I stop, at a loss for words, choked with emotion.

Bash lifts my quivering chin to gaze into my tired eyes. "No one has ever loved you, Sharie, the way I do."

CHAPTER TWENTY-TWO

By eight a.m., we shove out into the Gulf of Mexico. I meet Captain Pete, a friendly older gentleman. He tells me he will teach me to read all the dials and show me what all the switches mean in order to drive this yacht. The other two crew members come and introduce themselves as Tucker and Carlos. They show me where all kinds of supplies are stored.

First, the medical kits and other first-aid supplies. Then, foods: Canned goods and boxes full of all kinds of wonderful treats. A backup freezer below deck filled with meats and poultry of various cuts. I search through the cabinets, too, and find a lot of my favorite snacks, favorite wines, and beer. Carlos tells me one of his jobs is buying the groceries, and Mr. Devonshire had given him specific instructions for purchasing what I liked. I turn red with a smile. I feel a warm gush in my stomach.

I venture down to the master stateroom. My suitcase is there, ready for me to unpack. I open the closet, and already there are jeans, shirts, sweaters, shorts, and sundresses along with some sandals and a new pair of sneakers. I find a note:

Miss Sharie,

Mr. Devonshire requested that I go into town and purchase a few items of clothing for you. He provided me with your sizes and style preferences and indicated that you would prefer comfortable pieces for the journey. I hope they are to your liking and make your trip more enjoyable.

Carlos

I nod my head and chuckle. I hear a knock and turn to the doorway. Cornelia is standing there. "Am I interrupting?"

I smile. "No, not at all. I was just admiring the new clothes your son had Carlos get for me. I honestly just don't know what to say...and the office...did you see the office? I guess I'm not used to being handed things."

"My son loves you, Sharie, so you'd better get used to it," she says, patting my arm. "His father was just the same. I used to think I received so many lavish gifts because my husband worked so many hours and was away more than he was home. I thought it was a way for him to show love. But, friends of mine, their husbands weren't so generous with the gifts. I asked my husband about that one day when he came home with one of those fancy Aston Martin cars with my name on the license plate. I said, 'Charles, why on earth do you keep buying me gifts?' And you know what he said? 'Because you're my bride. My love. My heart. It makes me happy to see you smile.'"

"Oh God, that's so incredibly sweet. You and Bash must miss him terribly."

Cornelia has a small, faraway look on her face as if she is remembering a moment in time. For just a second, she is lost in a happy place; I can see it. She turns her eyes back to me.

"I do miss him. Sebastian is very much like him, too." She taps my back as a warm gesture. "Get settled, my dear, and then we'll raid the galley and get some grub." Before she steps out, she turns and adds, "Charles would have loved your spunk and cheeky demeanor. You've got fire, Sharie, and my son is a moth caught in your light. He is so very drawn to you, as am I." She smiles again and exits the room.

"Thanks!" I call out. I grin at Cornelia's kind words and warm essence. Most mothers are not very warm towards the women their sons choose. Or, the warmth takes time to build. Cornelia seems to have warmed up fast. But, taking into account all that has happened, I can probably see why she has.

"Sharie, is everything to your liking?" Bash asks, disturbing my thoughts.

I give him a big smile. "Yes, Bash! I can't believe all you've done for me. I am still shocked about the office. And Carlos! Truly, you didn't need to get me all of this." I wave my hand toward the closet.

"It's not too much. I just want you to be comfortable." He wraps me in his arms. "I really, truly love you, Sharie. It makes me happy to do these things for you." He kisses me tenderly, his desire spurring my own. I break the kiss before it gets too hot.

"Your mother is waiting for us in the galley. I suggest we resume this later."

218

Bash clears his throat. "Right. Good idea," he says, taking my hand and leading me to the galley for some of that grub his mother had mentioned.

***

The sun coming through the tiny portholes of the stateroom tell me it's morning. Still hazy, I'm a little confused as to how I got here, but I can feel how exhausted I am from the events of the day before, including spending all afternoon just getting settled on the ship. Last thing I can remember is dinner last night.

"Bash?" I call out, but I get no reply. I grab my robe and open the door. I feel the yacht moving as I make my way down the little hall and up the steps. I hear Bash and his mother talking, something about Bermuda. I find them in the main salon having tea.

"Good morning," I say quietly.

"Ah, there's my sleepyhead," Bash says.

I sit down next to him. "Yes, I don't remember much after dinner."

"You fell asleep on the lounger, dear, right after the meal. You've had such an ordeal the past two days, I'm surprised you're up and about at all. Bash carried you to bed."

I look at Bash, and he chuckles. "You were completely knackered, luv. You were snoring a bit, so I put you to bed." He smiles like a devil.

"Oh my God. I was?" I ask, putting my hands to my face.

"Well, I'm sure it was out of complete exhaustion. It was rather adorable. Now, would you care for some breakfast? There is also coffee, a pot made just for you."

"That sounds great."

Bash shows me to where the coffee, juice, and a plate of delicious foods are awaiting me, all in my newly-done office. My laptop is all hooked up and ready, too. "Bash, this couldn't be more perfect."

"Sit down. See how it feels; we might have to adjust the chair."

I pace over to the sturdy wooden desk and have a seat. I melt into the plush chair and swivel around to look out the windows. The sky is a vivid blue, and the ocean sparkles from the sun's rays. Immediately, I'm entranced, mesmerized by the tranquility of my scenery.

"This…is perfection." Bash hands me a mug of coffee made the way I like it, with one Splenda and cream.

"I take it you are happy with your arrangements then, Ms. Donovan?" he quips with his handsome smirk.

"Oh yes…I like. I like it a lot."

"Very well, then. You can properly thank me later." He winks. "I guess I'll leave you to work for a bit."

"I'm not sure how much work I'm going to get done," I mutter, glancing back at him. "Hey, before you go—I heard you and your mother talking about Bermuda. Are we stopping there?"

He strides over to my side behind the desk and moves the wireless mouse to my laptop. A picture of our excursion shows the path we are cruising.

"Yes, luv. See here." He points to the screen. "This dot is us. We are almost past Florida and into the Atlantic, now. We will cruise up and stay close to the coast of the Carolinas then head out towards Bermuda. It should take a couple days. There, we will refuel, get supplies, and drop Mother at the airport. She is flying back to England from there."

"Yeah…" I sigh. "Cornelia told me that, as much as she would love to, she wouldn't be able to do the whole trip."

"It's for the best," he says. "She needs to make preparations for houseguests and make arrangements at the family cemetery. She is very excited about having company. She has been lonely, especially since my father passed."

I turn towards Bash. "She told me she wanted to record all that has happened and make a family-history book to correct all the false rumors. I can help her with that, if she wants."

Bash leans down and lifts my chin to bring his lips to mine and kisses me. "She would love that, Sharie."

I peek at the screen again and point to the map of our trip. "This is really cool."

Bash nods. "Indeed. Every day you can check our progress. As we get closer to land, you will be able to spot that from miles away. So, I'll leave you to do some work. Have your breakfast. Enjoy your morning. I'll be at the helm with Captain Pete if you need me." He gives me a chaste kiss before going on his way.

I turn again in that wonderful chair and tilt back. The view is hypnotic, Bash is sexy as hell, and I'm on a beautiful yacht. How in the world am I ever going to get anything done?

***

Four days since we left the Gulf, we dock in Saint George, Bermuda. A limo already waits to take Cornelia to the airport. In a few moments, we are saying our goodbyes to her. She kisses Bash, then me. "I will see you in Devonshire. Have a wonderful journey." We watch her drive off. Captain Pete tells us we have the day to explore while they replenish the yacht's supplies for the rest of the trip.

Looking up at Bash, I smile. "I have never been to Bermuda. I wouldn't mind a little sightseeing."

He tucks my arm around his and gestures to the colorful island before us. "Your wish is my command," he says, escorting me off the yacht.

When I'm on land, I can still feel the sway of the ship in my legs. Bash tells me I will get used to it. We set out through Saint George Harbor and into a quaint, historic town. "This kind of reminds me of how historic New Orleans is," I say to Bash.

"It's just as old," he says. "British settlement officially began in 1612, but settlers were here years before that."

We wander around the narrow lanes that still retain their original names then go to King's Square and tour the National Trust Museum and the Unfinished Church.

Over on Ordnance Island, I take pictures of a replica of the ship *Deliverance* that sits right in the middle of everything. As the sun begins to set, an orange sky glows around us while we drink rum swizzles with a perfect meal at Wahoo's Bistro. The night is breezy, and stars light up the sky as we dine out on the patio overlooking the peaceful island.

"I wish we had more time here," I say wistfully to Bash. "I want to see more—it's so beautiful here."

"We will have to come back on holiday," he says. "Maybe after we are finished with our task and you're done with the book, we will come back and see the rest of Bermuda."

"I would love that. Good idea. Shouldn't be too long, now."

After dinner, we walk hand in hand back to the yacht. It's almost midnight, and Captain Pete has been wondering where we have been. We settle back on board. The engines purr to life, and we are once again moving out to sea. I am amazed at how many stars I see in the night sky and how bright they are.

I hear Bash stride up behind me.

"What has captured your attention out here, luv?"

I turn to him. "The stars. There are thousands of them. I never realized how clearly I could see them out on the ocean. They are so bright."

Bash puts his arms around me, his chest against my back, and snuggles me in the chilly air. "Stars can't shine without darkness." He turns me in his embrace and kisses me.

He picks me up and carries me to our stateroom. Without words, he undresses me first, then himself. He explores my body with hands and wet kisses until undercurrents of arousal heat me. I am begging him to love me. His eyes shine into mine as he enters my core. Tenderly, we make love. Then, with a fierceness of hunger and need, our passion builds. It becomes so strong that we shatter. My orgasm rocks me, hard. Bash rides it out with me cradled in his arms.

"You're going to be the death of me, Sharie," he chuckles, out of breath.

I smile. "I was thinking the same about you. The passion is so strong between us, I can't get enough. My body aches for you."

Leaning into my line of vision, I see his deep blue eyes, serious and searing into me even in the dim, golden light of our room. "I am all yours, Sharie. You own me."

I kiss him while I feel the stinging of warm tears in my eyes. No man has ever said that to me, and I know in my heart no other man ever will.

CHAPTER TWENTY-THREE

My days on the yacht are peaceful. I do some writing but still find time to learn about other aspects of life at sea, like how to fish, how to drive the yacht, how to read the radar. I also learn about weather patterns when, one day, we race around a storm so we won't rock or be subjected to rough seas. It is fascinating yet scary. I am told we will be docking in Devonshire in two days. A total of fifteen days' sailing, and I love every minute.

In the afternoon, I am able to call my sister from the yacht to tell her when we will be docking. She tells me of her flight arrangements. Soon, we will all be together.

***

The two days go fast, and Bash wakes me early this morning with tender kisses. "Good morning, luv. Get up and come with me. We are pulling in to Devon. I want you to see the coast."

I rise on my bare feet and grab my robe. Stepping out on the yacht's deck, my groggy-morning eyes start to focus on the landscape. Cliffs and sandy beaches line the shore. I see that other boats are already out on the water, fishing or getting ready to sail. Tiny cottages pepper the hillsides, lights in their windows glowing through the early-dawn fog. The air is fresh and cool as I take a deep breath. Bash is staring at me, smiling his cute smirk.

"What?" I ask, smiling back.

He raises an eyebrow. "The look on your face is priceless. I knew you would like it. Welcome to the English Riviera."

"Like it? No, Bash. This is exquisite. Charming. It's something out of dreams and fairytales."

He comes up from behind me and holds me in his arms.

"I want to show you so much of my home. I can't wait to share it all with you."

Bash and I stay on deck, having coffee, while Captain Pete docks us in. We dress and pack up our belongings to depart from the yacht. A Land Rover SUV is here to whisk us to Devonshire House, where Cornelia is awaiting our arrival.

About a twenty-minute drive later, we are going up a steep driveway, circling around to a front entrance. Bash opens the car door for me. I step out and look around. It's a palace. Plush, green grass rolls through acre after acre. Multi-colored flowers line the landscape. The house is situated on a cliff overlooking the sea, and I can still catch the scent of the saltwater in the breezy ocean air. I turn to the front door as Bash takes my hand and introduces me to two maids and a butler: Sarah, Edna, and Helmsley. The younger woman curtsies in front of me.

"Miss Sharie, I'm Sarah. I will be at your service for your stay at Devonshire House. I will be happy to get you anything you need."

I look at the young girl who seems so eager to please. "Thank you, Sarah. I'm sure I won't be much of a bother, though. You must forgive me; I am not used to having such attention."

"That's fine, miss. I will get your things situated."

"Welcome home, sir. How was the trip across the pond?" Helmsley asks Bash.

"Very well, thank you, Helms."

"Your mother is in the study, sir. She is most anxious to see you both."

Entering through a large wooden door into a foyer of marble tile, I follow Bash down a long hall. We enter a beautiful room. The study is a lovely, decorated library with maps and books and comfortable-looking lounge chairs. Tall windows from floor to ceiling on the far end overlook the English Channel that now has many more boats sailing than earlier this morning. I feel my mouth open in awe but quickly shut it when I hear the twinkle of Cornelia's voice.

"You have finally arrived!" she exclaims, coming over to us with her arms open wide. She hugs Bash, then me. "The rest of the trip was good with no incidents, I see."

I nod. "Yes, I think we were lucky we had smooth sailing and just one little storm."

Cornelia cocks her head to the side, giving me a sideways glance. "Yes...or just maybe you had a particular spirit watching over you?" she winks.

"You have a point," I say with a chuckle.

In a few minutes, Bash shows me to our room, which is decorated in a nautical theme in blues and deep greys. Rich, mahogany furniture fills the room, and of course, balcony doors open to a small-but-usable terrace that overlooks the deep-green yard and that wonderful shoreline. "I want you to be comfortable while you're here, Sharie. There are plenty of other rooms in the house for you to use if you want to work or be alone. I know how much you love your alone time."

I shake my head. "Bash, wherever you are, I'm comfortable. True, I do like my alone time, but it's getting better now. I don't mind being alone...with you."

He strides over to me, smoothly sealing his lips to mine. We are interrupted by Helmsley bringing us our suitcases followed by Sarah with a tray of tea and finger-sandwiches.

"Here you go, miss," Sarah chimes. "Some refreshments while you unpack. Dinner is at eight. Is there anything else we can get or do for you both?" Bash glances at me as if to ask me if I need anything.

"No, I'm fine, Sarah," I say, picking up a little snack from the tray. "Thank you."

Helmsley enters again. "The chest, sir—here or in the keeping room?"

"Here is fine," Bash tells him. "I will move it after dinner. Thanks. That will be all for us, for now."

I shake my head for the millionth time. "I don't know if I will get used to this."

Bash eyes me eating. "What—food?" he jokes.

I roll my eyes. "Ha, ha…No, maids, servants…It's a lot to take in. I feel a bit intimidated."

"Don't," he tells me. "They are here to basically run the house. After a while, you won't even know they're about. Helmsley and Edna have been with us for years. Mum hired Sarah a short time ago. Plus, my luv"—he grabs my chin—"you have a book to write. It's all going to work out, but first, shall we take care of this?" He taps his foot on the chest containing Prudence's remains.

***

We are siting around an elegant and formal table in an enormous dining hall. Paintings of landscapes with hounds and horses hang on towering walls, and large bay windows with lavish draperies done in gold and burgundy give the room a French-chateau feel.

My table at home can seat maybe ten, but this one is long enough for twenty. I am, however, very relaxed. Among what appears to be all grandeur, Bash and Cornelia are very down to earth and not as pretentious as their surroundings might suggest.

While we eat, Cornelia explains about the ceremony that will take place in two days at the family cemetery.

"I have called Father Thomas. All he knows is we have moved a relative to our family plot. Nothing more, nothing less. It begins at three p.m. and should not take more than a half-hour. I can't begin to tell you how grateful I am. Have you heard from your sister? When should we expect them?"

Swallowing the last bite of my second helping of mashed potatoes, I answer, "Charlotte, Jack, and the kids should be here by tomorrow afternoon. Bash is sending the SUV for them. They will stay for just the week. They can't leave the restaurant for too long."

Cornelia's sky-blue eyes twinkle as she smiles. "I am looking forward to some company around here. The little ones will love the beach. Oh—and they can see the horses, too!"

"Sounds wonderful, Cornelia. I'm sure we all will have a nice stay."

After dinner, Bash takes the chest and places it by the fireside in the keeping room. There are fresh cut flowers on either side. It reminds me of a small funeral parlor. I walk up to the chest and lay my hand on top. "You're almost home, Prudence," I whisper.

***

The next morning, Sarah enters my bedroom with a small tray. "Good morning, miss. Sleep well?"

"I did, Sarah. What do you have there?" I ask.

"Mr. Devonshire informed me you must have coffee first thing. There is all kinds of sugar and cream. Will you be joining the family for breakfast or having breakfast in your room this morning?"

I stare at her, wrapping my head around this new status quo. I must have startled her with the dumb look on my face. She puts her hands to her heart. "Miss Sharie, are you feeling all right? You look a bit off."

I blink and rub my forehead. "No, I'm fine...sorry," I chuckle. "I will be down for breakfast. Forgive me, Sarah. I am not used to having a servant or...people. I don't live like...or I...I'm not used to this."

Sarah smiles a pretty smile. "It's all right, miss. You will get used to it. I won't be under your feet too much. I'm just here to help, is all. Mr. Sebastian gave us orders to make sure you're comfortable."

I take a sip of coffee. "Not bad," I say, giving her a half-smile. "Sarah, please don't be offended—this may come off sounding a little rude—but having servants makes me sort of uncomfortable...Oh geesh, was that a crappy thing to say? I'm sorry...just not used to this. I don't know how to act, what to say!"

She laughs. "Oh, I like you very much already, miss. You will keep Mr. Sebastian on his toes." She reaches over and pats the bed. "It'll be fine. You're doing great. You will get used to it." She turns and straightens things up as she heads for the door.

"Yep, that's what I'm afraid of," I mutter under my breath.

After I finish my coffee and get dressed, I make my way through the halls and down the stairway. I spot Sarah, and she points me in the direction of an outside patio where Sebastian is reading the paper. "Hey," I say.

"Hello, luv." He stands to kiss me. "I rose early and didn't want to wake you." He motions with his hand toward the table. "Breakfast?"

"Yes, please," I say, taking the seat next to him. "Bash, can you show me where the cemetery is? I'd like to see it before the ceremony."

"Certainly, if that's what you'd like. I'll take you out there after you've eaten."

Out through the countryside and up a hill sits the small cemetery. It is here that Prudence will be at her final rest. As I walk along between the headstones, I see many Devonshires as well as other names on stones dating back to the 1600s. Some headstones are so worn I can barely make out the markings.

"Over here," Bash says, showing me the Ravensdale family row: Bernard, Suzette, Juliette, and Andrea. I read their headstones and recognize the epitaph Bash shared with me before:

Apart we are

be it centuries

We long to re-unite

in the hereafter.

There is already a hole dug and waiting for Prudence to lie alongside her family, to finally be at rest.

"Prudence needs a stone," I say softly to Bash.

"Mother and I agree. It has already been ordered, but with name and date only. We thought that you might like to write something special for it."

I look at Bash, my eyes wide in surprise. "I would be honored, but I don't feel worthy of that task." I shake my head. "I have no idea…I'm not sure I should—"

"Shhh…" Bash cuts in, putting both his hands on my upper arms. "You take all the time you need. It can be etched in whenever we want." With a kiss, he tells me, "I have faith something will come to you, and it will be great."

We stay for a few more minutes until Bash decides he wants to drive me through the area and show me around Devon, clear my head a bit. In a few hours, my sister will be here and we will be busy settling them in.

As we drive along, I spy places of interest that should be great sightseeing with Charlotte, Jack, and the kids. Bash also adds some attractions to my list that should make for a couple of nice days, including a picnic and horseback riding on the beach.

By the time we get home, Cornelia informs us my sister and everyone are on their way. Before long, they are pulling up in the driveway. The car doors open and the kids scramble out first. "Auntie Shreee!" Jaqueline squeals. I grab her up in my arms and kiss the smooth skin of her cheek. She clings to me like a monkey. Charlie gives me a fist bump and a big smile.

Jack and Charlotte climb out next and look exhausted. "Up since three a.m., but we made it!" she says.

"You will have plenty of time to catch up on sleep," I say, hugging her. "Come on inside."

We enter as Cornelia is coming out to greet them. Hugs and hellos go around. Helmsley approaches to take the bags, but Jack insists he doesn't need the help. I inform my brother-in-law it's what they do and that I am struggling to get used to it, too.

We show them to their rooms. Charlotte quickly opens her suitcase. "Sharie, come here," as she waves me over for a little privacy. "I met with Brandy before we left. She gave me this pouch full of stuff and some instructions for you."

My face is confused. "Instructions—for what?"

"She really didn't get into it with me, but she said she wrote it all down for you. Everything you will need for the burial."

"What?" I shot my sister a crazed look. "What's in here, Char?"

She shrugs. "I didn't look. I waited for you. All Brandy said was everything you need is written down and is in this bag."

I sit on the bed and unzip the pouch. There are five different-colored candles, some essence powder, a bundle of white sage, a small bottle of familiar green liquid, and a note.

Sharie,

This is important and must be done after the ceremony. When the moon is up, return to Prudence's grave with three

234

others. Give each a candle and place the white one in the ground above Prudence. Form a circle. Light the sage and candles—cleans the grave. Sprinkle the essence and offer everyone a sip of the absinthe I created specially for this ritual. Jaqueline's heart is pure and has the sight innocently, so if you include her in the ritual, give her sip to Prudence's grave. Then, recite the prayer. Only then can Prudence reunite and cross over.

I gaze at my sister. "Well?" she asks. "What does it say?"

"I...we, have to do some sort of ritual to help cross her over."

"Who's we?" she asks cautiously.

I wrinkle my nose at her. You, me, Jaqueline, and Cornelia would be my best guess."

"What do we have to do?"

"Nothing too unpleasant," I say hesitantly. "We just have to go back to the cemetery at night...when the moon is up...do a little sermon of our own."

Charlotte takes a deep breath, collapses next to me on the bed, and exhales. "Of course we do..." she comments, her voice dripping with sarcasm.

CHAPTER TWENTY-FOUR

The small funeral service for Prudence this afternoon goes smoothly. Father Thomas's reading is a short and sweet sermon welcoming a lost sister home. It's all very beautiful with white lilies and red roses everywhere.

I am pleased we have no negative incidents of any kind. I can only hope the special service I must do in a few hours will go just as smoothly.

Sitting at a local pub after the interment, we gather all around, talking of plans for the week ahead. It brings me back to the day we buried Mom, yet this time I am not as somber. No feelings of grief or sorrow. This time, I feel peace. Content that we put together a jigsaw puzzle that had a missing piece. Bash notices I am quiet and takes my hand.

"You all right, luv? You seem a little melancholy."

I give him a small smile. "I'm good," I answer, nodding my head. "I feel really good. She's back where she belongs."

He kisses my knuckles. "You made it happen," he whispers, gently lifting my chin with his fingers as his deep-blue eyes thoughtfully search mine. "You aren't worried about tonight, are you?"

"Maybe a little," I admit.

"You've got this, Sharie. I have no doubts. I will be right there. All of us will."

Everyone at the table gets quiet as they look to us. Jack raises his pint. "To Prudence!"

We all follow suit and lift our drinks. "To Prudence!"

***

The daylight shifts to dusk. I wait until the moon is vibrantly illuminated; its glow helps us as we travel through nightfall back to the cemetery. Bash, Jack, and Charlie hang back by the Range Rover while we girls return to Prudence's grave. Carrying a small flashlight, I open the pouch Brandy has sent to me. I pull out five candles: green, blue, yellow, pink, and finally the white one, which I stick into the soil on top of the grave.

"Form a circle," I say as I give out the remaining candles. My hands shake from nerves as I try to light the sage. Charlotte helps, and soon the sweet and savory smoke swarms above and around us. I have Lisette's pendant, and I now put it over my head. I light all the candles and sprinkle the powder. I take a deep breath. My heart is beating hard as I hesitate to do the rest.

"It's okay, Aunt Shree. She is waiting." Jacqueline holds her candle up as if to point at Prudence.

I let out a laugh on a breath of nerves. "You see her?" I ask.

"Yep. She's right over there. She is smiling."

I laugh again but tears follow. Cornelia and Charlotte look around. "I don't hear her," Cornelia whispers.

"She's not talkin'," Jaqueline says. "She's just waiting."

I wipe the wetness from my eyes and then a sniff of my nose. "Okay, Prudence…Here we go." Slowly, I uncork the absinthe. With shaky hands, I take a sip and pass it along to Charlotte, then to Cornelia. The little that is left Cornelia pours on the grave.

"We call the elements of earth, air, fire, and water to our circle. May the mighty winds of heaven bring us together in family. May the moon illuminate your way to the light and your new life."

As I read, the winds slowly shift and create a tunnel above our heads. A crack of thunder rumbles across the sky. Debris begins to blow all around, but the candles never go out. I read louder:

"Your time has finally come. Prudence, the angels will guide your spirit beyond this impasse. Go in peace. Be at peace forevermore on the other side."

The wind takes each colored candle's flame to intertwine them all, igniting a ring of fire that spins and swirls around us. The ring connects with the flame of the white candle then shoots straight up into a bright crack in a cloud. Too awestruck to move, I watch as a fiery tornado turns into a bright beam of light being pulled into the sky. A moment later, we are engulfed by a brilliant white light, but it does not hurt our eyes. The air suddenly calms and stills, making us feel suspended in gravity. Shadows move in the light and slowly come into focus. It's Prudence, and she is with many others. I see her family—we all do. All their lights made into one, each going up the lighted tunnel.

Before Prudence ascends, she comes close to me; I feel her essence touch my arm. It's warm. I can't truly see her as it's hard to focus around the brightness. She dims her light enough for me to see her image. Her smile is clear, and without a word she speaks. I hear her voice in my heart.

"Mademoiselle Sharie, you have freed me and I am home. Your kindness has been rewarded. Always remember, you are never alone."

She moves aside and I can feel my mother and father coming through the light. I can't see them, but I know they are there. The light surrounds me as if it is hugging me. I feel their presence and overwhelming joy. Somewhere in the light I also hear Cornelia call to her husband, Charles. Charlotte, Jaqueline, and I hold on to each other. Prudence's light gets brighter. As she enters the twirling beam, she turns back.

"Until someday in the hereafter…"

The winds pick up again, and the beam of light that lit the whole area starts to recede. Each shadow in the beam lifts up and away from us. We can feel its vacuum-like pull. Huddled all together, we watch. With another crack of thunder, it becomes as bright as daylight. And in a blink it is all gone, as if a light switch has been abruptly shut off. We all collapse to the ground. It suddenly seems so dark.

"Sharie!" Bash calls out, and we are swiftly in the light of flashlights. He grabs me into his arms. "Sharie! My God! I saw everything, but what happened?"

I raise my hands. "I'm okay. How is everyone else? Bash—your mother? Where is Cornelia?" I say, spinning my head.

"I'm right here," she says, taking my hand. "And I couldn't be better."

I hear my niece's giggles, the best sound in the world. "That was fun, Momma! Can we do that again?" she claps her hands.

Unanimously, the adults say "NO!" but laugh right along with her.

We collect the candles, brush ourselves off, and pile back into the car. Deep in our thoughts, no one talks, not one word is spoken on the drive home.

We arrive at Devonshire House as Sarah and Edna tell us there are tea and cookies in the keeping room. We each grab a teacup and a seat.

"Well, is one of you going to tell us about the light show?" Jack asks, raising his hands in the air, mimicking the lights.

"Prudence..." Cornelia softly says. "She was there, and so was your father, Sebastian. I felt him. He somehow let me know he is fine and he will be waiting for us to join him, someday. I am...speechless...but so very peaceful is the only way I can describe it."

Bash turns from his mother to me. "Is that what you saw?"

I nod my head. "Yeah, but I saw or maybe felt my parents' spirits. Prudence told us we're never really alone. I turn toward my sister. "You, too?"

She nods. "Yes, I felt them, too. They were in the light and they are happy." Jack reaches for her and holds her close.

"Jaqueline, you saw that, too?" I ask her.

"Yep. Grandma and Grandpa told me to be a good girl." She looks over to her brother. "They are angles! Did you see them, Charlie?"

"No." My nephew shakes his head. "I just saw lots of lightning or a fireball, I think. All of you looked like you were in a trance or something."

"Yes," Bash agrees. "We didn't see anything but a small stationary storm above all of you. We knew something had to be happening. I wasn't sure what. By the look on your faces, you have witnessed something from beyond the physical realm. A magical world? Or possibly, heaven. So I have to believe you all saw and felt what you claim."

"Love," I tell him. "We felt pure love."

***

In the following days, I notice changes in all of us. Nothing drastic, but in subtle ways we are more aware, more alive. My faith in many things has been restored.

We all seem closer, calmer. Something has shifted and balanced our perspectives. Worries have lessened and become almost insignificant. What once we ever feared is now no longer a burden. Bash and I seem more connected. I didn't think it could be possible to love each other stronger than we already did, but there is a closer attachment between us, now. Be it magical or spiritual, all of us have been touched forever.

***

I stay on in Devonshire after my sister and family leave. There is so much history and inspiration here that I find myself lost in my book. Days and nights blur into weeks that I spend writing *Ravensdale Manor*. Cornelia proofreads chapter after chapter, and I, in return, help her document a family-history book. I also know what I want to put on Prudence's headstone: *"Until someday in the hereafter..."* Those were her last words to me.

After finding out about my four-times great-grandfather who knew Prudence, Charlotte and I investigate our ancestry and collaborate on putting together a family-heritage book of our own to pass along. Even though we are an ocean apart, phone calls and videochatting are a weekly ritual.

I am having my coffee in bed this morning when my cell phone rings. It's Bash. "Hey, you," I say with a sleepy voice.

"Hello, luv. How are you this morning?"

"Good. When will you be home? I miss you. You've been away almost two weeks this time."

"Soon, luv. Just one more meeting and I'm on a plane and in your arms in no time."

Our conversation is interrupted by Sarah knocking on the door. "Miss Sharie, I have your breakfast."

Puzzled, I tell her to come in. "Funny, I don't remember telling you I was having breakfast in bed this morning, Sarah."

"Compliments of Mr. Sebastian, Miss."

I smile. "Bash, did you tell them to bring me breakfast in bed this morning?"

"I did. I hope you're happy with what I asked them to prepare."

Sarah sets a tray stand on the bed in front of me. There are a few red roses in a crystal vase and a silver dome covering a plate. I lift the cover. My eyes grow wide as I gasp with surprise! Nestled in a small white velvet box is the most beautiful diamond ring I've ever seen.

I hear Bash chuckle over the phone. "Sharie, look up."

I tilt my head—Bash stands in the doorway, cell phone still in hand. "Marry me."

~ *ONE YEAR LATER* ~

Standing on a stage behind a curtain, my palms begin to sweat as I concentrate on breathing. A stagehand informs me "Five minutes." I am still clueless as to how I ever got talked into speaking about my book in front of a filled auditorium in New York City. Bash takes my hands. "You've got this, luv. The book is becoming so popular. People love the story, and they will love you, too."

I swallow hard. "I feel like a fraud, Bash. I had help writing this story. Prudence gave it to me."

"Haven't your characters in your other books told you their stories? Prudence wanted this story told, too, and she chose you to tell it."

Nervous and antsy, I scratch the back of my neck. "I guess, but the book was written with magic."

"Stop looking for the magic, Sharie—you are it."

***

It has been a whirlwind year of book signings, public appearances, and interviews. All I can concentrate on now is walking up the aisle to Bash, to say I do. We decided to have our wedding in Devon at the historical Bickleigh Castle. Charlotte, my matron of honor, and Jaqueline as my flower girl make our special day complete. After a grand reception, our pre-packed bags are waiting for us on the *Dark Horse* as it sits ready to cruise us around Europe for our honeymoon.

After we've settled in on the yacht, Bash hands me a gift. "What's this?" I ask with surprise.

He shrugs "Not sure. It got here yesterday from the States. Open it up."

I take the shoebox-sized present, tear at the shiny white paper, and pull off the silver bow. I lift the lid, and there is a note:

Congratulations on your wedding. May heaven bless you both for many years. I replicated the original recipe. Enjoy with caution.

I reach in the box, removing bunches of tissue paper until I spot a wine-sized bottle containing a light-green liquid. On a tag attached to the neck it says:

Just one sip.

The label on the bottle…*"Absinthe"*…

The End

Crawfish Gumbo

1 stick of butter, melted

2cups chopped green onion

2 cups sliced okra

1/2 cup chopped white onion

3cups crawfish tails – chopped, if desired

2 cups raw oysters

1 cup chopped fresh tomato

2 cups tomato juice

1 1/2 quarts fish stock

3 Tbs. butter

3 Tbs. flour

1 Tbs. each of salt, ground black pepper, and ground cayenne pepper

3 cups cooked dirty rice

Sauté onions and okra with two tablespoons of the melted butter.

In a separate pot, put oysters, crawfish tails, tomatoes, tomato juice, and fish stock. Bring to a boil. When the onions and okra are soft, add to the pot of oysters and crawfish tails (gumbo).

In a small skillet, whisk the remaining butter and flour together over medium heat until brown. Blend this roux with the cayenne, salt, and black pepper, then add it to the pot of gumbo, stirring or whisking continuously until blended with the broth. Simmer for 90 minutes.

To serve, ladle about 2 cups gumbo over a mound of brown rice in each bowl.

Shrimp and Grits

Instant grits - about 1 cup.

2 Tbs. butter

2 ounces white cheddar cheese

4 slices pancetta bacon

1 cup chopped yellow onion

2 cloves garlic, minced

1/2 cup olive oil

1 to 1 1/2 pounds shrimp – cleaned and deveined. Or, buy pre-cooked frozen shrimp.

2 Tbs. parsley

Fry pancetta bacon till crispy. Remove from heat, drain, then chop.

Use about 3 Tbs. of the pancetta fat mixed with olive oil to sauté shrimp, onions, and garlic for a few minutes. Then, simmer on low heat, stirring occasionally, for another five minutes

Meanwhile, prepare grits according to package directions. When grits are done, incorporate into shrimp mixture. Turn heat to warm. Add chopped pancetta. Add cheese and butter and stir until melted.

To serve, spoon into bowls. Garnish with parsley.

* * *

Recipes for Absinthe Cocktails

from www.ABSINTHEONTHENET.com

The Atomic Bomb:

1/2 absinthe

1/2 brandy

Stir and pour

1/4 absinthe

1/4 tablespoon sugar

3/4 lemon juice

Knocked Out:

1 teaspoon white crème de Menthe

1/3 Absinthe

1/3 dry gin

1/3 French vermouth

Shake well, pout into cocktail glass.

La Fée Mimosa:

1 part absinthe

2 parts champagne

2 parts freshly squeezed orange juice

Absolution:

1 splash absinthe

2 splashes Krupnik (honey liquor)

3 splashes ginger cordial

Enjoy....Drink responsibly...

Author's Notes:

As always while writing my stories, music moves my creative force and is in the background. Songs that helped inspire *Absinthe*:

"Dark Horse" / Katie Perry

"Thinking Out Loud" / Ed Sheeran

"Fly" / Maddie & Tae

"Burn" / Ellie Goulding

"Secrets" / One Republic

Many have asked me, "Where do the ideas come from while you're writing?" or "How do you come up with ideas for your books?" Well, to be honest, some just really pop into my head out of the blue. I try not to question it. Sometimes, I see something or hear about something.

The I idea for Absinthe came to me one Saturday morning while watching the *History Channel*. I saw a segment about this mystical elixir and how it caused hallucinations. That was it. I grabbed a pen and my notebook and started writing notes, then a little outline. Before I knew it, the story had a mind of its own. I did a lot of research before typing away my days and nights as I always do. I found interesting facts, I used some real names and people, and I spun my fictional tale. Here is what I found:

Absinthe was created in the late 18th century by Dr. Pierre Ordinaire as an elixir for his patients in Couvet, Switzerland. Made with traditional herbs including wormwood, aniseed, fennel, star anise, hyssop, and lemon balm, the recipe truly did get into the hands of two sisters by the last name of Henriod who started selling it as a drink in the town and eventually sold it to a Major Dubied, whose daughter eventually married into the Pernod family.

The Pernods had opened a distillery in France and started producing absinthe. Under the name "Pernod Fils," they produced 30,000 liters of absinthe a day!

Absinthe had its heyday during the Golden Age of La Belle Époque in France. Unfortunately, it became associated with such drugs as heroin, cocaine, and cannabis and was accused of producing psychedelic effects. Prohibitionists, doctors, and wine producers who were upset with absinthe's popularity all ganged up against the production of the liquor and were able to persuade the French government to ban it in 1915.

Fortunately, absinthe has since been redeemed. Studies have shown that absinthe is no more harmful than any other liquor and that it does not induce hallucinations. The claims of the early 20th century are now seen as mass hysteria and falsehoods....Or are they?

Absinthe was legalized in the EU in 1988, and the USA has allowed various brands of absinthe to be sold within its borders since 2007.

So, those are some true facts about absinthe—A mythical, mysterious drink with an incredible history that has inspired many writers, poets, artists, and musicians. Van Gogh, Picasso, Hemmingway, and Wilde have all called Absinthe, also known as the Green Fairy, their muse.

This was a fun story to create. I hope you enjoyed the journey.

About the Author

Robin H. Soprano. Author of Contemporary Romance. Creating fictional worlds with magic and mystical paranormal hints. Spinning romantic adult fairytales.

Robin, born and raised in northern New Jersey, now lives in northeastern Florida with her husband and her black lab Corey.

Every day, she looks at her angels sitting on her desk, each holding special words…

Dream~ Wish~ Believe.

www.ingramcontent.com/pod-product-compliance
Lightning Source LLC
Chambersburg PA
CBHW071254250626
47159CB00004B/1185